Anonymous

# Dunigan's Six Cent Catholic Almanac and Laity's Directory

SALZWASSER VERLAG

**Anonymous**

# Dunigan's Six Cent Catholic Almanac and Laity's Directory

Reprint of the original, first published in 1859.

1st Edition 2023 | ISBN: 978-3-37513-420-4

Verlag (Publisher): Salzwasser Verlag GmbH, Zeilweg 44, 60439 Frankfurt, Deutschland
Vertretungsberechtigt (Authorized to represent): E. Roepke, Zeilweg 44, 60439 Frankfurt, Deutschland
Druck (Print): Books on Demand GmbH, In de Tarpen 42, 22848 Norderstedt, Deutschland

# DUNIGAN'S

### SIX CENT

# CATHOLIC ALMANAC

## And Laity's Directory,

### FOR THE YEAR OF OUR LORD

# 1859.

Of the Independence of the United States, the 84th.

## NEW YORK:
### EDWARD DUNIGAN & BROTHER,
### JAMES B. KIRKER,
#### 371 BROADWAY.
#### 1859.

# THE AMERICAN CATHOLIC ALMANAC:

# 1859.

## CHRONOLOGICAL CYCLES.

| | | | |
|---|---|---|---|
| Golden Number | 16 | Dominical Letter | C |
| Epact | 15 | Letter of the Martyrology | r |
| Solar Cycle | 19 | Julian Period | 6571 |

## EQUINOXES AND SOLSTICES.

| | | |
|---|---|---|
| Vernal Equinox | March 20 | Autumnal Equinox........Sept. 23 |
| Summer Solstice | June 21 | Winter Solstice..........Dec. 21 |

## MORNING STAR.

Venus will be Morning Star till September 27, and Evening Star after that time.

## ECLIPSES OF THE SUN.

I. Partial, February 2d. Invisible in this country.
II. Partial, March 4th. Invisible.
III. Partial, July 29th.
IV. Partial, August 28th. Invisible.

## ECLIPSES OF THE MOON.

I. Total, February 17th.
II. Total, August 13th. Invisible.

## HOLIDAYS OF OBLIGATION IN THE UNITED STATES.

| | | |
|---|---|---|
| Circumcision● | Jan. 1 | Whitsunday..............June 12 |
| Epiphany● | " 6 | Corpus Christi● ..........June 23 |
| Annunciation of B. V. M.●..M'ch 25 | | Assumption of the B. V. M...Aug. 15 |
| Easter | April 24 | All Saints ..............Nov. 1 |
| Ascension Day | June 2 | Christmas................Dec. 25 |

### ADDITIONAL HOLIDAYS OF OBLIGATION IN CANADA.

St. Peter and St. Paul......June 20 | Immaculate Conception ....Dec. 8

● Not of obligation in the dioceses in the limits of ancient Louisiana.

## FASTING DAYS IN THE UNITED STATES.

| | |
|---|---|
| Ash Wednesday..........March 9 | Vigil of the Assumption....Aug. 14 |
| All week-days in Lent, from | Ember Days........Sept. 21, 23, 24 |
| March 9 to April 23 | All Hallow Eve............Oct. 81 |
| Ember Days ......March 16, 18, 19 | Ember Days........Dec. 14, 16, 17 |
| Vigil of Pentecost ........June 11 | Fridays in Advent..Dec. 2, 9, 16, 23 |
| Ember Days.......June 15, 17, 18 | Christmas Eve.............Dec. 24 |

### ADDITIONAL FASTING DAYS IN CANADA.

Vigil of St. Peter & St. Paul..June 28 | Wednesdays in Advent, Dec. 7, 14, 21

### DAYS OF ABSTINENCE.

All the Fridays throughout the year.
Sundays in Lent, except where the Ordinary otherwise permits.

*N. B.*—Soldiers and sailors in the service of the United States, even in barracks, garrisons, &c., are dispensed, by an indult of Pope Pius IX., from the rule of abstinence, except on six days in each year, viz.: Ash Wednesday, Thursday, Friday, and Saturday in Holy Week, the Vigil of the Assumption, and Christmas Eve.

### EXPLANATION OF THE CALENDAR.

| | | | | | |
|---|---|---|---|---|---|
| Ap., App., | signifies | Apostle, Apostles. | D., | signifies | Doctor. |
| M., MM., | " | Martyr, Martyrs. | V., | " | Virgin. |
| P., | " | Pope. | W., | " | Widow. |
| A., | " | Abbot. | L., | -" | Lauds. |
| SS., | " | Saints. | M., | " | Mass. |
| H. G., | " | Holy Ghost. | Vesp., | " | Vespers. |
| H. M., | " | Holy Martyr, Mar- | Fol., | -" | Following. |
| HH. MM., | | tyrs. | Prec., | " | Preceding. |
| B., | " | Bishop. | Com., | " | Commemoration. |
| C., | " | Confessor. | Fer., | " | Feria. |

### COLOR OF VESTMENTS WORN IN THE HOLY SACRIFICE OF THE MASS.

*White* is used on the festivals of our Lord, of the B. Virgin Mary, and of all the saints who are not martyrs.

The *Red* is used on Pentecost, on the Finding and Exaltation of the Cross, and on the feasts of the Apostles and Martyrs, except the Holy Innocents.

The *Purple* or *Violet*, which is the penitential color, is used on all the Sundays and Ferias of Advent, and during the whole of the penitential time from Septuagesima Sunday till Easter; as also on all Vigils, Ember Days, and Rogation Days, when the office is of them, and on Dec. 28th.

The *Green* is used on all Sundays and Ferias from Trinity Sunday to Advent exclusively, and from the octave of the Epiphany to Septuagesima Sunday exclusively, when the office is of the Sunday; but in the Paschal time the White is used.

The *Black* is used on Good Friday, and in Masses of *Requiem* for the dead; which may be said on any day that is not a Sunday or a double, except from Palm Sunday to Low Sunday, and during the octaves of Christmas, of the Epiphany, of Pentecost, and of Corpus Christi.

| D. M. | DAY OF WEEK. | COLOR. | PROPER OF THE UNITED STATES. |
|---|---|---|---|
| 1 | Satur | † W | CIRCUMCISION OF OUR LORD (*Holyday of obligation*), d. 2d cl. Gl. Cr. Pref. and *Communic.* of Nativ. In Vesp. com. of fol. only. |
| 2 | Sund | † R | (Vacant.) Octave of St. Stephen, d. com. of St. John and H. Innocents in L. and M. Gl. Cr. and Pref. of Nativ. V. from ch. of fol. com. of prec. and H. Innocents. |
| 3 | Mond | † W | Octave of St. John Ap. d. com. of H. Innocents in L. and M. Gl. Cr. Pref. of App. In Vesp. com. of fol. |
| 4 | Tues | † R | Octave of H. Innocents, doub. Gl. Pref. of Nativ. In Vesp. com. of fol. and St. Telesphorus. |
| 5 | Wed | † W | Vigil of Epiphany, semid. as on Circumcision, com. of St. in L. and M. 3d coll. *Deus qui salutis.* Gl. Pref. of Nativ. |
| 6 | Thurs | † W | EPIPHANY OF OUR LORD (*Holyday of oblig.*), d. 1st cl. with Oct. Gl. Cr. Pref. and *Communic.* prop. during the Oct. Vesp. of same. |
| 7 | Frid | W | Second day in Oct. semid. 2d coll. *Deus qui.* 3d *Eccl.* or *pro Papa.* Gl. &c. as yest. Vesp. of Oct. *Abstinence.* |
| 8 | Satur | W | Third day in Oct. semid. as yest. Vesp. from ch. of fol. com. of Oct. (ant. *Lux.* V. omnes.) |
| 9 | Sund | W | Within Oct. semid. office as on Epiph. (1st noct. in Epist. 1 Corinth.) Com. Oct. in L. and M. V. as on Epiph. com. Oct. |
| 10 | Mond | W | Fifth day in Oct. semid. as 7th inst. Vesp. com. of St. Hyginus. |
| 11 | Tues | W | Sixth day in Oct. semid. as on 7th inst. Com. of St. in L. and M. Vesp. of Oct. |
| 12 | Wed | W | Seventh day in Oct. semid. as on 7th inst. Vesp. of fol. |
| 13 | Thurs | W | Octave of Epiph. doub. as in prop. In V. com. of fol. and St. Felix. |
| 14 | Frid | W | St. Hilary, B. C. D. doub. (hym. ch.) 9th less. and com. of St. in L. and M. Gl. Cr. Pref. com. Vesp. from ch. of fol. (hymn ch.) com. of prec. and St. Maur. *Abstinence.†* |
| 15 | Satur | W | St. Paul, 1st hermit, C. doub. 9th less. and com. of St. in L. and M. Gl. Vesp. of fol. com. of preced. and 2d S. after Epiph. |
| 16 | Sund | W | Second after Epiph. Holy Name of Jesus, 9th less. and com. of Sund. in L. and M. Gl. Cr. Pref. of Nativ. and last Gosp. of Sund. In Vesp. com. of Sund. and fol. |
| 17 | Mond | W | St. Anthony, Ab. doub. Gl. Vesp. of fol. com. of St. Paul, preced. and St. Prisca. |
| 18 | Tues | W | St. Peter's chair at Rome, gr. doub. 9th less. of St. Prisca. Com. of St. Paul and St. Prisca in L. and M. Vesp. com. of St. Paul, fol. and St. Marius and comp. |
| 19 | Wed | R | St. Canute, M. semid. *ad lib.*, at Lauds, *suffrages of Saints*, 9th less. and com. of SS. in L. and M. 3d coll. *Deus qui.* Gl. Vesp. of fol. com. of prec. |
| 20 | Thurs | R | SS. Fab. and Sebast. MM. doub. Gl. Vesp. from ch. of fol. com. of prec. |
| 21 | Frid | R | St. Agnes, V. M. doub. Gl. In Vesp. com. of fol. *Abstinence.* |
| 22 | Satur | R | SS. Vincent and Anastasius, MM. semid. 2d coll. *Deus qui*, 3d church or Pope. Vesp. of fol. com. of Sund. and St. Emerentiana. |
| 23 | Sund | W | Third after Epiph. Espousal of B. V. Mary, gr. doub. 9th less. of Sund. com. of Sund. and St. in L. and M. Gl. Cr. Pref. *te in despona.* last Gosp. of Sund. Vesp. com. of fol. and Sund. |
| 24 | Mond | R | St. Timothy, B. M. doub. Gl. Vesp. of fol. com. of St. Peter, prec. |
| 25 | Tues | W | Conversion of St. Paul, Ap. gr. doub. com. of St. Peter in L. and M. Gl. Cr. Pref. App. In Vesp. com. of St. Peter. |
| 26 | Wed | R | St. Polycarp, B. M. doub. Vesp. from ch. of fol. (hymn ch.) com. of prec. |
| 27 | Thurs | W | St. John Chrysostom, B. C. D. doub. Gl. Cr. In Vesp. com. of fol. and St. Agnes. |
| 28 | Frid | R | St. Marcellus (from 16th) P. M. semid. 9th less. and com. of St. in L. and M. Gl. 3d coll. of B. V. Mary. Vesp. of fol. (hymn ch.) com. of prec. *Abstinence.* |
| 29 | Satur | W | St. Francis of Sales, B. C. doub. Gl. In Vesp. com. of Sund. |
| 30 | Sund | G | Fourth Sund. after Epiph. of the Sund. semid. Gl. Cr. 3d coll. of B. V. Mary, 3d for church or Pope. Vesp. of fol. com. of Sund. |
| 31 | Mond | W | St. Peter Nolasco, C. doub. Gl. Vesp. from ch. of fol. com. of prec. |

* Consecration of Archbishop of New York.*
† Consecration of Bishop of Vincennes.

1st Month. **JANUARY, 1859.** 31 Days.

| MOON'S PHASES. | | BOSTON. | NEW YORK. | BALTIMORE. | CHARLESTON. |
|---|---|---|---|---|
| | | H. M. | H. M. | H. M. | H. M. |
| New Moon | 4th | 0 42 mo. | 0 30 mo. | 0 20 mo. | 0 6 mo. |
| First Quarter | 12th | 2 89 mo. | 2 27 mo. | 2 17 mo. | 2 8 mo. |
| Full Moon | 18th | 7 5 ev. | 6 58 ev. | 6 48 ev. | 6 80 ev. |
| Third Quarter | 25th | 4 1 ev. | 8 49 ev. | 8 89 ev. | 8 26 ev. |

| Day of Month. | Day of Week. | ANNIVERSARIES, &c. |
|---|---|---|
| 1 | Sa | New Year's Day |
| 2 | S | Assassination of Mgr. Sibour |
| 3 | M | Battle of Princeton, 1777 |
| 4 | Tu | Mrs. Seton dies, 1821 |
| 5 | W | Twelfth Day |
| 6 | Th | Archbishop Hughes consecrated, 1838 |
| 7 | Fr | Battle of New Orleans |
| 8 | Sa | |
| 9 | S | First after Epiphany |
| 10 | M | |
| 11 | Tu | Bishop Challoner dies, 1781 |
| 12 | W | Sist. Marg. Bourgeoys dies, 1706 |
| 13 | Th | |
| 14 | Fr | |
| 15 | Sa | |
| 16 | S | Second after Epiphany |
| 17 | M | St. Anthony dies, 356 |
| 18 | Tu | |
| 19 | W | |
| 20 | Th | |
| 21 | Fr | Creeks defeated, 1814 |
| 22 | Sa | |
| 23 | S | Third after Epiphany |
| 24 | M | |
| 25 | Tu | |
| 26 | W | |
| 27 | Th | |
| 28 | Fr | |
| 29 | Sa | |
| 30 | S | Fourth after Epiphany |
| 31 | M | |

| D. M. | DAY OF WEEK. | COLOR. | PROPER OF THE UNITED STATES. |
|---|---|---|---|
| 1 | Tues | R | St. Ignatius, B. M. doub. Vesp. of fol. com. of prec. |
| 2 | Wed | † W | Purification of B. V. M. doub. 2d cl. (Candles are blessed before Mass.) Gl. Cr. Pref. of Nativ. In Vesp. com. of fol. and St. Blaize. At Complin *Ave Regina.* |
| 3 | Thurs | † W | St. Raymund de Pennafort, C. doub. (hymn ch.) 9th less. com. of St. Bláize in L. and M. Gl. Vesp. from ch. of fol. (hymn ch.) com. of prec. |
| 4 | Frid | † W | St. Andrew Corsini, B. C. doub. (hymn ch.) Gl. Vesp. from ch. of fol. com. of prec. *Abstinence.* |
| 5 | Satur | † R | St. Agatha, V. M. doub. Gl. Vesp. from ch. of fol. com. of prec. of Sund. and St. Dorothea. |
| 6 | SUND | † W | Fifth Sunday after Epiphany. St. Titus, B. C. doub. 9th less. of Sund. com. of Sund. and St. Dorothea in L. and M. last Gosp. of Sund. Vesp. from ch. of fol. (hymn ch.) com. of prec. and Sund. |
| 7 | Mond | † W | St. Romuald, Abb. doub. Vesp. from ch. of fol. com. of prec. |
| 8 | Tues | † W | St. John of Matha, C. doub. and St. Apollonia, V. M. In Vesp. com. of fol. (ant. *Simile.* V. dif.) |
| 9 | Wed | † R | St. Martina, V. M. semid. 9th less. and com. of St. Apollonia in L. (ant. Veni V. Specie) and M. 3d coll. *A Cunctis.* Vesp. of fol. com. of prec. |
| 10 | Thurs | W | St. Scholastica, V. doub. Gl. Vesp. of Same. |
| 11 | Frid | G | Feria. 2d coll. *Fidelium,* 3d *A Cunctis.* Vesp. of fol. *Abstinence.* |
| 12 | Satur | W | Office of Immaculate Conception of B. V. M. semid. 2d coll. of the Holy Ghost, 3d for ch. or P. Gl. Pref. *et te in Com. Concep. Immac.* Vesp. from ch. of fol. com. of prec. |
| 13 | SUND | G | Sixth Sunday after Epiph. of the Sund. semid. 2d coll. *A Cunctis,* 3d *ad lib.* In Vesp. com. of fol. |
| 14 | Mond | R | St. Valentine, M. *Simp.* Gl. 2d coll. *Fidelium,* 3d coll. *A Cunctis.* Vesp. from ch. of fol. |
| 15 | Tues | R | SS. Faustin and Jovita, MM. Simp. 2d coll. *Fidelium,* 3d *A Cunctis.* Vesp. of feria. |
| 16 | Wed | G | Feria. 2d coll. *Fidelium,* 3d *A Cunctis.* Vesp. of fol. |
| 17 | Thurs | W | Office of the M. B. Sacrament, semid. 2d coll. *A Cunctis,* 3d *ad lib.* Gl. Pref. of Nativ. Vesp. of same, com. of fol. |
| 18 | Frid | R | St. Simeon, B. M. Simp. 2d coll. *Fidelium,* 3d coll. *A Cunctis.* Vesp. of fol. *Abstinence.* |
| 19 | Satur | W | Office of Immaculate Conception of B. V. M. semid. 2d coll. de Sp. Sancto, 3d Eccl. or pro Papa, Pref. of B. V. M. Vesp. from ch. of fol. com. of prec. (*Benedicamus Dno.* with double Alleluia, which is not said again until Holy Saturday; in its place, say *Laus tibi Dne.*) |
| 20 | SUND | P | Septuagesima Sunday, semid. as in prop. 2d coll. *A Cunctis,* 3d *ad lib.* Cr. Pref. of Trin. Vesp. of Sund. |
| 21 | Mond | P | Feria. 2d coll. *Fidelium,* 3d *A Cunctis.* Vesp. of fol. com. of St. Paul. |
| 22 | Tues | W | St. Peter's Chair at Antioch, gr. doub. Vesp. com. of St. Paul and fol. |
| 23 | Wed | W | St. Peter Damian, B. C. D. doub. 9th less. and com. of Vigil of St. Mathias in L. and M. (In medio.) Gl. Cr. and last Gosp. of Vig. Vesp. of fol. com. of prec. |
| 24 | Thurs | R | St. Mathias, Ap. doub. 2d cl. Gl. Cr. Pref. of App. Vesp. of same. |
| 25 | Frid | P | Feria. 2d coll. *Fidelium,* 3d coll. *A Cunctis.* Vesp. of fol. *Abstinence.* |
| 26 | Satur | W | Office of Immaculate Conception of B. V. M. semid. 2d coll. de Sp. Sancto, 3d Eccl. or pro Papa, Pref. of B. V. Vesp. from ch. of fol. com. of prec. |
| 27 | SUND | P | Sexagesima Sunday. Semid. as in prop. 2d coll. *A Cunctis,* 3d *ad lib.* Cr. Pref. of Trin. Vesp. of same. |
| 28 | Mond | P | Feria. 2d coll. *Fidelium,* 3d *A Cunctis.* Vesp. feria. |

| 2d Month. | FEBRUARY, 1859. | 28 Days. |
|---|---|---|

| MOON'S PHASES. | BOSTON. | NEW YORK. | BALTIMORE. | CHARLESTON. |
|---|---|---|---|---|
| | H. M. | H. M. | H. M. | H. M. |
| New Moon ........ 2d | 8 20 ev. | 8 8 ev. | 7 58 ev. | 7 45 ev. |
| First Quarter ...... 10th | 2 56 ev. | 2 44 ev. | 2 34 ev. | 2 21 ev. |
| Full Moon ......... 17th | 5 58 mo. | 5 46 mo. | 5 36 mo. | 5 23 mo. |
| Third Quarter ..... 24th | 9 38 mo. | 9 26 mo. | 9 16 mo. | 9 2 mo. |

ANNIVERSARIES, &c.

St. Bridget.

Treaty of Guadalupe Hidalgo, 1848.

Bp. Connolly died, 1825.

Michael Angelo died, 1564.

Washington born, 1789.

| D. M. | DAY OF WEEK. | COLOR. | PROPER OF THE UNITED STATES. |
|---|---|---|---|
| 1 | Tues | P | Feria. Coll. 2d *Fidelium*, 3d *A Cunctis*. Vesp. of same. |
| 2 | Wed | P | Feria. Coll. as yest. Vesp. of fol.* |
| 3 | Thurs | W | Office of the M. B. Sacrament, semid. 2d coll. *A Cunctis*, 3d *ad lib.* Gl. Pref. of Nativ. Vesp. from ch. of fol. com. of prec. and St. Lucius, P. and M. |
| 4 | Frid | W | St. Casimir, C. semid. com. St. Lucius in L. and M. 3d coll. *A Cunctis.* Vesp. from ch. of fol. *Abstinence.* |
| 5 | Satur | W | Office of Immaculate Conception of B. V. M., semid. 2d coll. *de Sp. Sancto*, 3d *Eccl.* or *pro Papa*, Pref. of B. V. Vesp. from ch. of fol. com. of preced. |
| 6 | SUND | P | Quinquagesima Sunday, semid. as in prop. 2d coll. *A Cunctis*, 3d *ad lib.* Cr. Pref. of Trin. Vesp. of fol. com. of Sund. and SS. Perpetua and Felicitas. |
| 7 | Mond | W | St. Thomas Aquinas, C. D. doub. com. of SS. in L. and M. Gl. Cr. Vesp. from ch. of fol. |
| 8 | Tues | W | St. John of God, doub. Vesp. of same. |
| 9 | Wed | P | Ash Wednesday, Pref. of Lent. Vesp. of fol. com. of feria.‡ |
| 10 | Thurs | R | The Forty Martyrs, semid. less. 1st Noct. *Debitores*, 9th less. and com. of feria in L. and M. 3d coll. *A Cunctis.* Gl. and last Gosp. of feria. Vesp. of fol. com. of prec. and foria. |
| 11 | Frid | R | Most Sacred Passion of our Lord, gr. doub. *all lib.* 9th less. and com of feria in Lauds, Gloria, 2d coll. of feria, Pref. of Cross, last Gosp. of feria. Vesp. com. of fol. and feria. |
| 12 | Satur | W | St. Gregory I., P. C. D. doub. less. 1st Noct. *Sapiens.* 9th less. and com. of feria in L. and M. Gl. Cr. and last Gosp. of feria. In Vesp. com. of Sund.§ |
| 13 | SUND | †P | First Sunday of Lent, semid. coll. as in prop. Cr. Vesp. of fol. com. of Sund. |
| 14 | Mond | †W | St. Frances, Wid. (11th inst.) doub. less. 1st Noct. *Mulierem*, 9th less. and com. of feria in L. and M. Gl. and last Gosp. of feria. Vesp. of same, com. of feria. |
| 15 | Tues | †P | Feria. Coll. as Sund. Vesp. of feria. |
| 16 | Wed | †P | Emb. day, semid. and prop. coll. as yest. Vesp. of fol. com. of feria. |
| 17 | Thurs | †W | St. Patrick, B. C. doub. less. 1st Noct. *Fidelis sermo*, 9th less. and com. of feria in L. and M. Gl. and last Gosp. of feria. Vesp. of fol. com. of prec. and feria. |
| 18 | Frid | †W | Emb. day, St. Gabriel Arch., gr. doub. 9th less. and com. of feria in L. and M. Gl. Cr. last Gosp. of feria. Vesp. of fol. com. of prec. and feria. |
| 19 | Satur | †W | St. Joseph, C. Spouse of B. V. M., doub. 2d cl. (8th and 9th less. in one.) 9th less. and com. of feria in L. and M. Gl. (Cr. in patronal church) and last Gosp. of feria. In Vesp. com. of Sund. Ember day.‖ |
| 20 | SUND | †P | Second Sunday of Lent, semid. as in prop. Cr. Vesp. of fol. com. of Sund. |
| 21 | Mond | W | St. Benedict, Ab. doub. less. 1st Noct. *Laudemus*, 9th less. and com. of feria in L. and M. Gl. and last Gosp. of feria. Vesp. of fol. com. of prec. and feria.¶ |
| 22 | Tues | W | Most Holy Crown, gt. doub. *ad lib.* 9th less. of feria, com. of feria, in L. and M. Gl. Cr. Pref. *de Cruce*, last Gosp. of feria. In Vesp. com. of feria. |
| 23 | Wed | P | Feria. Coll. as Sund. Vesp. of same. |
| 24 | Thurs | P | Feria. As yest. Vesp. of fol. com. of feria.** |
| 25 | Frid | †W | ANNUNCIATION OF THE B. V. MARY, doub. 2d cl. (*Holyday of oblig.*) 8th and 9th less. in one, 9th less. and com. of feria in L. and M. Gl. Cr. Pref. *Et te in Annunc.* and last Gosp. of feria. (At High-mass, all kneel during the words *Et incarnatus est.*) In Vesp. com. of fol. in feria. |
| 26 | Satur | †R | Office of the Spear and Nails of our Lord, gr. doub. *ad lib.* 9th less. and com. of feria in L. and M. Gl. Cr. Pref. *de Cruce* and last. Gosp. of feria. In Vesp. com. of Sund. |
| 27 | SUND | †P | Third Sunday of Lent, semid. as in prop. Cr. Vesp. of same. |
| 28 | Mond | †P | Feria. Coll. as on Sund. Vesp. of same. |
| 29 | Tues | †P | Feria. Coll. as yest. Vesp. of same. |
| 30 | Wed | †P | Feria. Coll. as yest. Vesp. of same. |
| 31 | Thurs | †P | Feria. Coll. as yest. Vesp. of same. |

\* Consecration of Bishop of Philadelphia.
‡ Do.     do.     Albany.
§ Do.     do.     Monterey.
‖ Do.     do.     Milwaukee.
¶ Do.     do.     Wheeling.
** Do.     do.     Boston.

# 3d Month.  MARCH, 1859.  31 Days.

| MOON'S PHASES. | BOSTON. | NEW YORK. | BALTIMORE. | CHARLESTON. |
|---|---|---|---|---|
| | H. M. | H. M. | H. M. | H. M. |
| New Moon ........ 4th | 2 26 ev. | 2 14 ev. | 2 4 ev. | 1 51 ev. |
| First Quarter ...... 11th | 11 56 ev. | 11 44 ev. | 11 34 ev. | 11 20 ev. |
| Full Moon ......... 18th | 5 1 ev. | 4 49 ev. | 4 39 ev. | 4 26 ev. |
| Third Quarter...... 26th | 4 42 mo. | 4 30 mo. | 4 20 mo. | 4 6 mo. |

ANNIVERSARIES, &c.

| Day of Week | Day of Month | Anniversaries |
|---|---|---|
| Tu | 1 | Independence of Texas, 1836. |
| W | 2 | |
| Th | 3 | Arrival of Maryland settlers, 1634. |
| Fr | 4 | |
| Sa | 5 | |
| 8 | 6 | |
| M | 7 | |
| Tu | 8 | |
| W | 9 | Ash-Wednesday ········ |
| Th | 10 | |
| Fr | 11 | |
| Sa | 12 | |
| 8 | 13 | |
| M | 14 | Reception of Mrs. Seton, 1805. |
| Tu | 15 | |
| W | 16 | Death of Father Brebeuf, 1649. |
| Th | 17 | |
| Fr | 18 | |
| Sa | 19 | |
| 8 | 20 | La Salle assassinated, 1685. |
| M | 21 | |
| Tu | 22 | |
| W | 23 | |
| Th | 24 | |
| Fr | 25 | |
| Sa | 26 | |
| 8 | 27 | St. Mary's founded, 1634. |
| M | 28 | Ursuline Convent, Quebec, founded, 1639. |
| Tu | 29 | |
| W | 30 | |
| Th | 31 | |

| D. M. | Day of Week. | Color. | PROPER OF THE UNITED STATES. |
|---|---|---|---|
| 1 | Frid | †R | Office of the Five Wounds of our Lord, gr. doub. *ad lib.* 9th less. and com. of feria in L. and M. Gl. Cr, Pref. *de Cruce* and last Gosp. of feria. In Vesp. com. of fol. and feria. |
| 2 | Satur | W | St. Francis of Paula, C. doub. less. 1st Noct. *Beatus vir.* 9th less. and com. of feria in L. and M. Gl. and last Gosp. of feria. Vesp. of same, com. of Sund. (*To-morrow the altar is adorned with flowers.*) |
| 8 | Sund | P | Fourth Sunday of Lent, semid. as in proper. Cr. Vesp. of fol. com. of Sund. |
| 4 | Mond | W | St. Isidore, B. C. D. doub. less. 1st Noct. *Sapient.* 9th less. and com. of feria in L. and M. Gl. Cr. and last Gosp. of feria. Vesp. from ch. of fol. com. of prec. and feria. |
| 5 | Tues | W | St. Vincent Ferrier, C. doub. less. 1st Noct. *Beatus vir.* 9th less. com. of feria in L. and M. Gl. last Gosp. of feria. In Vesp. com. of feria. |
| 6 | Wed | P | Feria. Coll. as Sund. Vesp. of feria. |
| 7 | Thurs | P | Feria. Coll. as yest. Vesp. of feria. |
| 8 | Frid | R | Office of the Most Precious Blood of our Lord, gr. doub. *ad lib.* 9th less. and com. of feria in L. and M. Gl. Cr. Pref. *de Cruce* and last Gosp. of feria. In Vesp. com. of feria. |
| 9 | Satur | P | Feria. Vesp. from ch. of fol. (*Crucifixes and pictures are veiled before Vespers.*) |
| 10 | Sund | P | Passion Sunday, semid. 2d coll. *Eccl.* or *pro Papa,* Cr. Pref. *de Cruce,* which is said daily unless otherwise marked. Vesp. of fol. com. of Sund. |
| 11 | Mond | W | St. Leo, P. C. D. doub. less. 1st Noct. in prop. 9th less. of feria com. of feria in L. and M. Gl. Cr. Vesp. com. of feria. |
| 12 | Tues | P | Feria. Coll. as Sund. Vesp. of fol. com. of feria. |
| 18 | Wed | R | St. Hermenegild, M. semid. less. 1st Noct. *Fratres Debitores.* 9th less. of feria com. of feria in L. and M. 3d Orat. *Eccl.* or *pro Papa,* 2d Gosp. of feria. In Vesp. com. of feria, St. Tiburtius and Comp. |
| 14 | Thurs | P | Feria. Coll. as on Sund. Vesp. of same.* |
| 15 | Frid | W | Seven Dolors of the B. V. M., gr. doub. 9th less. and com. of feria in L. and M. Gl. Cr. Pref. *Et te in Transfixione,* and last Gosp. of feria. Vesp. com. of fol. and feria. |
| 16 | Satur | P | Feria. Coll. as on Sund. Vesp. from ch. of Sund. com. of St. Anicetus, P. M. |
| 17 | Sund | P | Palm Sunday, All prop. com. of St. Anicetus in L. *only.* (*Blessing and distribution of Palms.*) Cr. Vesp. of same. |
| 18 | Mond | P | Feria. Ant. prop. at Lauds, 2d coll. *Eccl.* or *pro Papa.* |
| 19 | Tues | P | Feria. Ant. prop. at Lauds. At Mass as yest. *Passion* from St. Mark. |
| 20 | Wed | P | Feria. Ant. prop. In Mass as yest. *Passion* from St. Luke. *Tenebræ.* |
| 21 | Thurs | W | Maundy Thursday, doub. 1st cl. All prop. *Tenebræ.* |
| 22 | Frid | B | Good Friday, doub. 1st cl. All proper. *Passion* from St. John. *Tenebræ.* |
| 28 | Satur | W | Holy Saturday, doub. 1st cl. All proper. Vesp. of fol. as in Missal and Brev. At Complin, *Regina Cæli.* |
| 24 | Sund | W | Easter Sunday, doub. 1st. cl. with Oct. All prop. Gl. Cr. with Pref. and *Communic.* prop. during the Oct. |
| 25 | Mond | W | Easter Monday, doub. 1st cl. as yest. and in prop. (After Lauds is recited the Litany of the Saints, *kneeling.*) |
| 26 | Tues | W | Easter Tuesday, doub. 1st. cl. as yest. and in prop. |
| 27 | Wed | W | Of the Oct. semid. 2d coll. *Eccl.* or *pro Papa.* Vesp. of Oct. com. of St. Vitalis, M. |
| 28 | Thurs | W | Of the Oct. semid. as yest. com. of St. Vitalis (without lesson), in Laud. and Mass. (3d coll. not said.) Vesp. of Oct. |
| 29 | Frid | W | Of the Oct. semid. as 27th inst. and in prop. Vesp. of Oct. *Abstinence.* |
| 80 | Satur | W | Of the Oct. semid. as 27th inst. and in prop. Vesp. of fol. |

* Consecration of Bishops of Hartford and Charleston.

| MOON'S PHASES. | | BOSTON. | NEW YORK. | BALTIMORE. | CHARLESTON. |
|---|---|---|---|---|---|
| | | H. M. | H. M. | H. M. | H. M. |
| New Moon | 8d | 5 33 mo. | 5 21 mo. | 5 11 mo. | 4 48 mo. |
| First Quarter | 10th | 6 37 mo. | 6 25 mo. | 6 15 mo. | 6 2 mo. |
| Full Moon | 17th | 4 22 mo. | 4 10 mo. | 4 0 mo. | 3 47 mo. |
| Third Quarter | 24th | 0 1 mo. | 11 49 ev. | 11 39 ev. | 11 26 ev. |

| Day of Week. | Day of Month. | ANNIVERSARIES, &c. | BOSTON; New England, N.Y. State, Mich'n, Wisconsin, Iowa, & Oregon. Sun rises. | Sun sets. | Moon rises. | N. YORK CITY; Phila., Conn., N. Jer., Penn., Ohio, Indiana, and Illinois. Sun rises. | Sun sets. | Moon rises. | WASHINGTON; Maryl'nd, Vir- ginia, Kent'ky, Missouri, and California. Sun rises. | Sun sets. | Moon rises. | CHARLES'N; N. Carol'a, Tenn., Georgia, Ala., Mississippi, and Louisiana. Sun rises. | Sun sets. | Moon rises. |
|---|---|---|---|---|---|---|---|---|---|---|---|---|---|---|

Anniversaries, &c. (partial):
- 3 St. Patrick's 1st Baptism
- Baltimore made a Metropolitan See, 1808.
- La Salle discovers mouth of Mississippi, 1683
- Leopold Association founded, 1829
- Third Council of Baltimore, 1837.
- English College, Rome, founded, 1579
- Easter. Bishop Concanen consecrated, 1808
- Louisiana ceded, 1803

| D. M. | DAY OF WEEK. | COLOR. | PROPER OF THE UNITED STATES. |
|---|---|---|---|
| 1 | Sund | W | Low Sunday, doub. Gl. Cr. Pref. of Paschal Time, which is said daily unless otherwise marked. In Vesp. com. of fol. |
| 2 | Mond | W | St. Athanasius, B. C. D. doub. less. 1st Noct. Act. Gl. Cr. Vesp. of fol.* |
| 3 | Tues | R | Finding of the Holy Cross, doub. 2d cl. 9th less. com. of SS. Alexander and Comp. MM. in L. and M. Vesp. com. of fol. |
| 4 | Wed | W | St. Monica, Wid. doub. less. 1st Noct. *Fratres.* Vesp. from ch. of fol. hymn ch. com. of prec. |
| 5 | Thurs | W | St. Pius V. P. C. doub. Vesp. of fol. com. of prec. |
| 6 | Frid | R | St. John before the Latin Gate, gr. doub. less. 1st. Noct. Ep. St. John as on Sund. Within Oct. of Ascens. Vesp. com. of fol. |
| 7 | Satur | R | St. Stanislaus, B. M. doub. Vesp. of fol. com. of prec. and Sund. |
| 8 | Sund | W | Second Sunday after Easter. Apparition of St. Michael, gr. doub. 9th less. Sund. com. of Sund. in L. and M. Vesp. com. of fol. and Sund. |
| 9 | Mond | W | St. Gregory Nazianzen, B. C. D. doub. Vesp. from ch. of fol. com. of prec. and St. Gordian and Comp. |
| 10 | Tues | W | St. Antoninus, B. C. doub. 9th less. and com. of SS. in L. and M. Vesp. of fol. |
| 11 | Wed | R | St. Mark (from April 25), Evan. doub. 2d cl. Gl. Cr. Pref. of Ap. In Vesp. com. of fol. |
| 12 | Thurs | R | St. Nereus and Comp., MM. semid. Gl. 2d coll. *Conceds.* 3d *Eccl.* or *pro Papa.* Vesp. of fol. |
| 13 | Frid | R | St. Philip and St. James (from 1st), App. doub. of 2d cl. less. 1st Noct. from 4th Sund. after Easter. Gl. Cr. Pref. of Apos. In Vesp. com. of fol. and St. Boniface, M. *Abstinence.* |
| 14 | Satur | W | St. Anselm (from April 21) B. C. D. doub. 1st Noct. *Sapientiam,* 9th less. of St. com. of St. in L. and M. Gl. Cr. In Vesp. com. of fol. and Sund. |
| 15 | Sund | W | Third Sunday after Easter. Patronage of St. Joseph, doub. 2d cl. in prop. 9th less. of Sund. com. of Sund. in L. and M. last Gosp. of Sund. Vesp. com. of Sund. and fol. |
| 16 | Mond | W | St. Ubaldus, B. C. semid. less. 1st Noct. *lib. Apoc.* 2d coll. *Conceds,* 3d *Eccl.* or *pro Papa.* Vesp. of fol. com. of prec. |
| 17 | Tues | W | St. Paschal Baylon, C. doub. Vesp. from ch. of fol. com. of prec. |
| 18 | Wed | R | St. Venantius, M. doub. Vesp. from ch. of fol. com. of prec. and St. Pudentiana. |
| 19 | Thurs | W | St. Peter Celestine, P. C. doub. 9th. less. of V. M. com. of V. M. in L. and M. In Vesp. com. of fol. |
| 20 | Frid | W | St. Bernardine of Sienna, C. semid. 2d coll. *Conceds,* 3d *Eccl.* or *pro Papa.* Vesp. of fol. com. of prec. *Abstinence.* |
| 21 | Satur | R | St. Fidelis of Sigmaringen (from April 24), M. doub. Vesp. from ch. of fol. com. of prec. and Sund. |
| 22 | Sund | R | Fourth Sunday after Easter. St. John Nepomucene, M. doub. 9th less. of Sund. com of Sund. in L. and M. Vesp. from ch. of fol. com. of prec. and Sund. |
| 23 | Mond | R | St. Peter, Martyr (from April 29), doub. Vesp. of fol. com. of prec. |
| 24 | Tues | W | Our Blessed Lady, Help of Christians, gt. doub. In Vesp. com. of fol. and St. Urban. P. and M. |
| 25 | Wed | W | St. Gregory VII., P. and. C. doub. 9th less. of St. com. of St. in L. and M. Vesp. from ch. of fol. com. of prec. and St. Eleutherius, P. and M. |
| 26 | Thurs | W | St. Philip Neri, C. doub. 9th less. of St. com. of St. in L. and M. In Vesp. com. of fol. and St. John, P. M. |
| 27 | Frid | W | St. Mary Magdalen of Pazzi, V. semid. 9th less. of St. com. of St. in L. and M. 3d coll. *Conceds.* Vesp. of fol. com. of prec. *Abstinence.* |
| 28 | Satur | W | St. Catharine of Sienna, (from April 30) doub. In Vesp. com. of Sund. |
| 29 | Sund | W | Fifth Sunday after Easter, semid. in proper. In Vesp. com. of fol. and St. Felix, P. M. |
| 30 | Mond | R | Rogation. St. Soter and Caius, PP. MM. semid. (from April 22) less. 1st Noct. *Fratres Debitores,* 9th less. of Rog. com. of Rog. and St. in L. and M. last Gosp. of feria. Vesp. from ch. of fol. com. of prec. and St. Petronilla, V. (Litanies said after Lauds on the three Rogation days.) |
| 31 | Tues | R | Rogation. St. George, M. semid. (from April 23) less. 1st Noct. *Scrip. occur,* com. of St. Petronilla in L. and M. 3d coll. of Rogation. Vesp. from ch. of fol. com. of prec. |

\* Consecration of the Bishop of Dubuque.

| MOON'S PHASES. | | BOSTON. | NEW YORK. | BALTIMORE. | CHARLESTON. |
|---|---|---|---|---|---|
| | | H. M. | H. M. | H. M. | H. M. |
| New Moon | 2d | 5 20 ev. | 5 8 ev. | 5 4 ev. | 4 45 ev. |
| First Quarter | 9th | 0 15 ev. | 0 8 ev. | 11 59 mo. | 11 40 mo. |
| Full Moon | 16th | 4 23 ev. | 4 11 ev. | 4 6 ev. | 3 47 ev. |
| Third Quarter | 24th | 6 5 ev. | 5 58 ev. | 5 49 ev. | 5 30 ev. |

| Day of Month | Day of Week | ANNIVERSARIES, &c. |
|---|---|---|
| 1 | Su | |
| 2 | M | Association for the Prop. of the Faith, 1822 |
| 3 | Tu | |
| 4 | W | Ticonderoga taken, 1775 |
| 5 | Th | Napoleon died, 1821 |
| 6 | Fr | Seventh Council of Baltimore, 1849 |
| 7 | Sa | |
| 8 | Su | St. Michael's and St. Augustine's burnt, 1844 |
| 9 | M | Plenary Council of Baltimore, 1852 |
| 10 | Tu | Sixth Council of Baltimore, 1846 |
| 11 | W | |
| 12 | Th | |
| 13 | Fr | Jamestown founded, 1607 |
| 14 | Sa | Fifth Council of Baltimore, 1843 |
| 15 | Su | Rev. Alban Butler died, 1773 |
| 16 | M | Daniel O'Connell died, 1847 |
| 17 | Tu | Fourth Council of Baltimore, 1840 |
| 18 | W | |
| 19 | Th | |
| 20 | Fr | Death of F. Marquette, 1675 |
| 21 | Sa | |
| 22 | Su | |
| 23 | M | |
| 24 | Tu | First Ordination in the United States, 1793 |
| 25 | W | |
| 26 | Th | |
| 27 | Fr | |
| 28 | Sa | Trappists embark for America, 1808 |
| 29 | Su | De Soto lands in Florida, 1539 |
| 30 | M | |
| 31 | Tu | |

| D. M. | DAY OF WEEK. | COLOR. | PROPER OF THE UNITED STATES. |
|---|---|---|---|
| 1 | Wed | R | Rogation and Vigil. SS. Cletus and Marcellinus, PP. and MM. semid. (Ap. 26) less. 1st Noct. *Fratres Debitores*, 9th less. of Vigil, com. of Vigil in L. and M. 8d coll. Rog. last Gosp. of Vigil. Vesp. of fol. |
| 2 | Thurs | W | ASCENSION OF OUR LORD (*Holyday of oblig.*), doub. 1st cl. Vesp. of same. |
| 8 | Frid | W | Of the Oct. semid. 2d coll. *Concede*, 8d *Eccl.* or *pro Papa.* Vesp. of Oct. |
| 4 | Satur | W | Of the Oct. semid. 2d coll. *Concede*, 8d Ecc. v. P. Vesp. from ch. of fol. Sund. com. of Oct. |
| 5 | SUND | W | Sunday within the Octave, semid. 2d coll. of Oct. Vesp. of fol. com. of Sund. and Oct. |
| 6 | Mond | W | St. Norbert, B. and C. doub. com. of Oct. in L. and M. Gl. Cr. Pref. of Ascension.- In Vesp. com. of Oct. |
| 7 | Tues | W | Of Octave, as on 8d inst. Vesp. of Oct. |
| 8 | Wed | W | Of Octave, as yest. Vesp. of fol. com. of SS. Primus and Felicianus. |
| 9 | Thurs | W | Octave of Ascension, doub. as on feast and prop. 9th less. of SS. com. of SS. in L. and M. In Vesp. com. of fol. |
| 10 | Frid | W | St. Margaret, Queen of Scots, W. semid. com. of 6th feria in L. and M. 3d coll. *Concede*, Pref. of Ascension. In Vesp. com. of feria. *Abstinence.* |
| 11 | Satur | P | Vigil of Pentecost (fast), semid. as on Sund. within Oct. except. prop. less., prayers not said at prime. One coll. Pref. and com. prop. Vesp. of fol. |
| 12 | SUND | † R | Whitsunday, doub. 1st cl. Vesp. of same. |
| 13 | Mond | † R | Whitmonday, doub. 1st cl. Vesp. of Oct. |
| 14 | Tues | † R | Whittuesday, doub. 1st cl. Vesp. of Oct. |
| 15 | Wed | † R | (Fast) Ember day of the Octave, semid. com. of SS. Vit. and Comp. in L. and M. Vesp. of Oct. |
| 16 | Thurs | † R | Of the Octave, semid. 2d coll. *Eccl.* or *pro Papa.* Vesp. of Oct. |
| 17 | Frid | † R | (Fast) of Octave, semid. 2d coll. *pro Papa.* Vesp. of Oct. com. of SS. Mark and Marcellianus, MM. |
| 18 | Satur | † R | (Fast) Ember day of the Octave, semid. com. of SS. in L. and M. Vesp. of fol. com. of 1st Sund. after Pent. (After none Paschal time ends.) |
| -19 | SUND | † W | Trinity Sunday (1st after Pent.), doub. 2d cl. 9th less. com. of Sund. in L. 2d coll. of Sund. last Gosp. of Sund. Vesp. com. of fol. of Sund. and of St. Silverius, P. and M. |
| 20 | Mond | † W | St. Barnabas, gr. doub. (from 11th) 9th less. of St. com. of St. in L. and M. Gl. Cr. Pref. of Apos. In Vesp. com. of St. Aloysius. |
| 21 | Tues | † W | St. Aloysius Gonzaga, C. doub. 2d coll. *pro Papa.* Vesp. from ch. of fol. com. of prec. and St. Paulinus. |
| 22 | Wed | † W | (Vigil) St. John *a Facunda* (from 12) doub. 9th less. of St. com. of St. in L. and M. Vesp. of fol. |
| 23 | Thurs | † W | SOLEMNITY OF CORPUS CHRISTI (*Holyday of obligation*), doub. 1st cl. with Oct. all prop. Gl. Cr. Pref. of Nativ. (which is said daily in Oct. unless otherwise marked). In vesp. com. of fol. |
| 24 | Frid | † W | Nativity of St. John Baptist, doub. 1st cl. with Oct. com. of Oct. Corp. Christi in L. and M. In Vesp. com. of fol. and Oct. Corp. Christi. *Abst.* |
| 25 | Satur | † W | St. William, Abbot, doub. com. of Oct. Corp. Christi, and St. John Bap. in L. and M. Vesp. from ch. of fol. com. of prec. Oct. of Corp. Christi and St. John Bap. |
| 26 | SUND | † W | Second Sunday after Pent. SS. John and Paul, doub. 9th less. of Sund. com. of Sund. of Oct. Corp. Christi, and St. John Bap. in L. and M. last Gosp. of Sund. Vesp. com. of Sund. of Oct. of Corp. Christi and St. John Bap. |
| 27 | Mond | † W | Of the Octave of Corpus Christi, semid. com. of Oct. of St. John Bap. in L. and M. 8d coll. *Concede.* In Vesp. com. of Oct. of St. John Bap.● |
| 28 | Tues | † W | (Vigil) of Octave of Corpus Christi, semid. 9th less. of Vigil, com. of Oct. of St. John Bap. and Vigil in L. and M. last Gosp. of Vigil. Vesp. of fol. com. of Oct. of Corp. Christi and St. John Bap. |
| 29 | Wed | † R | SS. Peter and Paul, doub. 1st cl. com. of Oct. of Corp. Christi in L. and M. Pref. of Apostles. In Vesp. com. of Oct. of Corp. Christi. |
| 30 | Thurs | † W | Octave of Corpus Christi, com. of Oct. of St. John Bap. and Apostles in L. and M. Pref. of Nativ. In Vesp. com. of Oct. of St. John Baptist and Apostles. |

**6th Month.**     # JUNE, 1859.     **30 Days.**

| MOON'S PHASES. | | BOSTON. | NEW YORK. | BALTIMORE. | CHARLESTON. |
|---|---|---|---|---|---|
| | | H. M. | H. M. | H. M. | H. M. |
| New Moon | 1st | 2 26 mo. | 2 14 mo. | 2 4 mo. | 1 51 mo. |
| First Quarter | 7th | 6 4 ev. | 5 52 ev. | 5 42 ev. | 5 28 ev. |
| Full Moon | 15th | 5 34 mo. | 5 22 mo. | 5 12 mo. | 4 59 mo. |
| Third Quarter | 28d | 9 48 mo. | 9 36 mo. | 9 26 mo. | 9 18 mo. |
| New Moon | 30th | 9 57 mo. | 9 45 mo. | 9 35 mo. | 9 22 mo. |

**ANNIVERSARIES, &c.**

| Day of Month | Day of Week | |
|---|---|---|
| 1 | W | Pope Gregory XVI. died, 1846 |
| 2 | Th | Ascension Day |
| 3 | Fr | |
| 4 | Sa | Oblates, Balt., founded, 1825 |
| 5 | M | |
| 6 | M | |
| 7 | Tu | Robert Bruce dies, 1329 |
| 8 | W | Corner-stone of old St. Patrick's laid, 1809 |
| 9 | Th | Rev. J. Carroll, Pref. Apostolic, 1784 |
| 10 | Fr | |
| 11 | Sa | Whitsunday |
| 12 | M | Steamer Pennsylvania destroyed, 1858 |
| 13 | M | Father Kohlmann's case, 1813 |
| 14 | Tu | |
| 15 | W | Accession of Pius IX., 1846 |
| 16 | Th | Bunker Hill, 1776 |
| 17 | Fr | War declared, 1812 |
| 18 | Sa | See of Cincinnati established, 1821 |
| 19 | M | |
| 20 | M | |
| 21 | Tu | Cardinal Fisher beheaded, 1535 |
| 22 | W | Corpus Christi |
| 23 | Th | St. John's College, Fordham, opens, 184— |
| 24 | Fr | |
| 25 | Sa | Father Cancer killed, 1547 |
| 26 | M | San Francisco founded, 1776 |
| 27 | M | |
| 28 | Tu | |
| 29 | W | St. Peter and St. Paul |
| 30 | Th | |

| D. M. | DAY OF WEEK. | COLOR. | PROPER OF THE UNITED STATES. |
|---|---|---|---|
| 1 | Frid | † W | Octave of St. John Baptist, com. of Oct. of App. in L. and M. Pref. of App. Vesp. of fol. com. of prec. and Octave of App. and of SS. Processus and Martinianus. *Abstinence.* |
| 2 | Satur | † W | Visitation of B. V. Mary, gr. doub. 9th less. of SS. com. of Oct. of App. and of SS. in L. and M. Gl. and Cr. Pref. of B. V. M. In Vesp. com. of Sund. and Oct. of App. |
| 3 | SUND | † R | Third after Pent. The Most Precious Blood of our Lord, doub. 2d cl. 9th less. and com. of Sund. in L. and M. Gl. Cr. Pref. *de Cruce* and last Gosp. of Sund. (High Mass of SS. Peter and Paul, com. of Precious Blood and Sund. Pref. of App.) In Vesp. com. of fol. and Sund. |
| 4 | Mond | † W | Feast of the Most Sacred Heart of Jesus (July 1), com. of Oct. in L. and M. gr. doub. Pref. *de Cruce.* In Vesp. com. of fol. and of Oct. of App. |
| 5 | Tues | † W | Com. of St. Paul, Ap. doub. (from June 30) com. of St. Peter in L. and M. Vesp. of the Oct. |
| 6 | Wed | † R | Octave of St. Peter and St. Paul. Vesp. from ch. of fol. com. of prec. |
| 7 | Thurs | W | St. Leo, P. and C. semid. (hymn ch.) (from June 28) 2d Orat. *A Cunctis,* 3d *ad lib.* Vesp. from ch. of fol. com. of prec. |
| 8 | Frid | W | St. Elizabeth, Wid. semid. 2d coll. *A Cunctis,* 3d *ad lib.* Vesp. of fol. com. of prec. *Abstinence.* |
| 9 | Satur | W | St. Anthony of Padua (from June 13), doub. (hymn ch.) In Vesp. com. of Sund. |
| 10 | SUND | G | Fourth Sunday after Pent., semid. 2d coll. *A Cunctis,* 3d *ad lib.* Vesp. of fol. com. of Sund. and St. Pius, P. and M. |
| 11 | Mond | W | St. Basil, Great, B. C. (June 14) doub. 9th less. of S. com. of St. in L. and M. Vesp. from ch. of fol. com. of prec. |
| 12 | Tues | W | St. John Gualbert, Abbot, doub. Vesp. com. of fol. |
| 13 | Wed | R | St. Anacetus, P. M. semid. coll. as 8th inst. Gl. Vesp. of fol. com. of prec. |
| 14 | Thurs | W | St. Bonaventura, B. C. D. 1st Noct. *Sapientiam.* Gl. Cr. Vesp. com. of fol. |
| 15 | Frid | W | St. Henry, C. semid. (hymn ch.) coll. as 7th inst. Gl. Vesp. of fol. com. of prec. *Abstinence.* |
| 16 | Satur | W | Our Lady of Mount Carmel, gr. doub. Gl. Cr. Pref. *Et te in Commem.* In Vesp. com. of Sund. |
| 17 | SUND | G | Fifth after Pent., 2d coll. *A Cunctis,* 3d *ad lib.* Vesp. of fol. and SS. Symphora, &c. |
| 18 | Mond | W | St. Camillus *de Lellis,* C. doub. 9th less. and com. of SS. in L. and M. Gl. Vesp. from ch. of fol. (hymn ch.) com. of prec. |
| 19 | Tues | W | St. Vincent of Paul, C. doub. Gl. Vesp. from ch. of fol. com. of prec. and St. Margaret. |
| 20 | Wed | W | St. Jerome Æmilian, C. doub. com. of St. in L. and M. Gl. In Vesp. com. of fol. and St. Praxedes. |
| 21 | Thurs | W | St. John Francis Regis, C. doub. (hymn ch.) (June 16) 9th less. of St. in L. and M. Vesp. from ch. of fol. com. of prec. |
| 22 | Frid | W | St. Mary Magdalen, Penit. doub. Gl. Cr. Vesp. from ch. of fol. com. of prec. and St. Liborius. *Abstinence.* |
| 23 | Satur | R | St. Appollonaris, M. doub. com. of Vigil and St. in L. and M. last Gosp. of Vigil. In Vesp. com. of Sund. and St. Christina. |
| 24 | SUND | G | Sixth Sunday after Pent., semid. com. St. in L. and M. 3d coll. *A Cunctis.* Vesp. of fol. |
| 25 | Mond | R | St. James, Ap. doub. 2d. cl. com. of St. Christopher in L. and M. Gl. Cr. Pref. of App. In Vesp. com. of fol. |
| 26 | Tues | W | St. Anne, Mother of B. V. M. gr. doub. Gl. In Vesp. com. of fol. and St. Pantaleon, M. |
| 27 | Wed | W | St. Juliana, V. (June 19) doub. 9th less. of St. com. of St. in L. and M. In Vesp. com. of fol. |
| 28 | Thurs | R | SS. Nazarius and Compan., MM. semid. coll. as 7th inst. Gl. Vesp. from ch. of fol. com. of prec. and SS. Felix, &c. |
| 29 | Frid | W | St. Martha, V. semid. com. of SS. in L. and M. 3d coll. *A Cunctis.* Gl. Vesp. of fol. com. of prec. and SS. Abdon, &c. *Abstinence.*\* |
| 30 | Satur | R | St. Irenæus, B. M. (June 28) doub. 9th less. of SS. com. of SS. in L. and M. Vesp. from ch. of fol. com. of prec. and S. |
| 31 | SUND | W | Seventh Sunday after Pent. St. Ignatius, doub. 9th less. of Sund. com. of Sund. in L. and M. Gl. Cr. Pref. of Trin. Vesp. of fol. com. of St. Paul, prec. and Sund. (In Dioc. Balt. doub. 1st cl. with Oct.) |

\* Transl. of Abp. Alemany.

**7th Month.** # JULY, 1859. **31 Days.**

| MOON'S PHASES. | | BOSTON. | NEW YORK. | BALTIMORE. | CHARLESTON. |
|---|---|---|---|---|---|
| | | H. M. | H. M. | H. M. | H. M. |
| First Quarter | 7th | 1 10 mo. | 0 58 mo. | 0 48 mo. | 0 35 mo. |
| Full Moon | 14th | 8 9 ev. | 7 57 ev. | 7 47 ev. | 7 34 ev. |
| Third Quarter | 21st | 10 44 ev. | 10 33 ev. | 10 22 ev. | 10 9 ev. |
| New Moon | 29th | 5 0 ev. | 4 48 ev. | 4 38 ev. | 4 25 ev. |

| Day of Month. | Day of Week. | ANNIVERSARIES, &c. | BOSTON; NEW ENGLAND, N. Y. STATE, MICHI'N, WISCONSIN, IOWA, & OREGON. | | | N. YORK CITY; PHILA., CONN., N. JER., PENN., OHIO, INDIANA, AND ILLINOIS. | | | WASHINGTON; MARYL'ND, VIRGINIA, KENT'KY, MISSOURI, AND CALIFORNIA. | | | CHARLES'N; N. CAROL'A, TENN., GEORGIA, ALA., MISSISSIPPI, AND LOUISIANA. | | |
|---|---|---|---|---|---|---|---|---|---|---|---|---|---|---|
| | | | Sun rises. | Sun sets. | Moon rises. | Sun rises. | Sun sets. | Moon sets. | Sun rises. | Sun sets. | Moon sets. | Sun rises. | Sun sets. | Moon sets. |
| | | | H. M. | H. M. | H. M. | H. M. | H. M. | H. M. | H. M. | H. M. | H. M. | H. M. | H. M. | H. M. |
| 1 | Fr | | 4 26 | 7 40 | 8 55 | 4 31 | 7 35 | 8 50 | 4 37 | 7 29 | 8 45 | 4 55 | 7 11 | 8 29 |
| 2 | Sa | Visitation of the B. V.. Virginia disc., 1584. | 4 26 | 7 40 | 9 35 | 4 32 | 7 35 | 9 31 | 4 37 | 7 29 | 9 27 | 4 55 | 7 11 | 9 16 |
| 3 | S | Quebec founded, 1608 | 4 27 | 7 40 | 10 1 | 4 32 | 7 35 | 9 59 | 4 38 | 7 29 | 9 57 | 4 56 | 7 11 | 9 50 |
| 4 | M | Declaration of Independence, 1776 | 4 27 | 7 39 | 10 26 | 4 33 | 7 34 | 10 25 | 4 38 | 7 28 | 10 25 | 4 56 | 7 11 | 10 22 |
| 5 | Tu | Second Native revolt, Philadelphia, 1844 | 4 28 | 7 39 | 10 49 | 4 33 | 7 34 | 10 49 | 4 39 | 7 28 | 10 50 | 4 57 | 7 11 | 10 52 |
| 6 | W | | 4 29 | 7 39 | 11 10 | 4 34 | 7 34 | 11 12 | 4 40 | 7 28 | 11 14 | 4 57 | 7 11 | 11 21 |
| 7 | Th | | 4 29 | 7 39 | 11 35 | 4 34 | 7 34 | 11 38 | 4 40 | 7 28 | 11 42 | 4 58 | 7 11 | 11 52 |
| 8 | Fr | | 4 30 | 7 38 | morn. | 4 35 | 7 33 | morn. | 4 41 | 7 27 | morn. | 4 58 | 7 10 | morn. |
| 9 | Sa | Beaujeu defeats Braddock, 1755 | 4 31 | 7 38 | 0 3 | 4 36 | 7 33 | 0 7 | 4 42 | 7 27 | 0 12 | 4 59 | 7 10 | 0 26 |
| 10 | S | | 4 31 | 7 38 | 0 35 | 4 37 | 7 33 | 0 40 | 4 42 | 7 27 | 0 46 | 5 0 | 7 10 | 1 4 |
| 11 | M | | 4 32 | 7 37 | 1 13 | 4 38 | 7 32 | 1 19 | 4 43 | 7 26 | 1 26 | 5 0 | 7 10 | 1 46 |
| 12 | Tu | | 4 33 | 7 37 | 2 1 | 4 39 | 7 32 | 2 8 | 4 44 | 7 26 | 2 15 | 5 1 | 7 9 | 2 36 |
| 13 | W | | 4 34 | 7 36 | 2 55 | 4 39 | 7 31 | 3 2 | 4 45 | 7 25 | 3 9 | 5 1 | 7 9 | 3 30 |
| 14 | Th | | 4 35 | 7 36 | rises. | 4 40 | 7 31 | rises. | 4 45 | 7 25 | rises. | 5 2 | 7 9 | rises. |
| 15 | Fr | | 4 36 | 7 35 | 8 13 | 4 41 | 7 30 | 8 8 | 4 46 | 7 24 | 8 3 | 5 3 | 7 8 | 7 48 |
| 16 | Sa | | 4 37 | 7 34 | 8 39 | 4 42 | 7 29 | 8 35 | 4 47 | 7 24 | 8 31 | 5 3 | 7 8 | 8 20 |
| 17 | S | | 4 38 | 7 34 | 9 0 | 4 43 | 7 29 | 8 57 | 4 48 | 7 23 | 8 55 | 5 4 | 7 8 | 8 47 |
| 18 | M | | 4 39 | 7 33 | 9 18 | 4 43 | 7 28 | 9 16 | 4 49 | 7 23 | 9 15 | 5 4 | 7 7 | 9 11 |
| 19 | Tu | N. Y., N. Orl., and Cinn. made Metrop's, 1850 | 4 39 | 7 32 | 9 38 | 4 44 | 7 27 | 9 38 | 4 50 | 7 22 | 9 37 | 5 5 | 7 7 | 9 37 |
| 20 | W | St. Louis made Metropolitan, 1847 | 4 40 | 7 32 | 9 57 | 4 45 | 7 27 | 9 58 | 4 50 | 7 22 | 9 59 | 5 5 | 7 6 | 10 8 |
| 21 | Th | | 4 41 | 7 31 | 10 17 | 4 46 | 7 26 | 10 19 | 4 51 | 7 21 | 10 22 | 5 6 | 7 6 | 10 29 |
| 22 | Fr | | 4 42 | 7 30 | 10 40 | 4 47 | 7 25 | 10 44 | 4 52 | 7 20 | 10 48 | 5 7 | 7 5 | 10 59 |
| 23 | Sa | | 4 43 | 7 29 | 11 9 | 4 48 | 7 24 | 11 14 | 4 53 | 7 19 | 11 19 | 5 7 | 7 5 | 11 34 |
| 24 | S | Oregon made a Metropolitan, 1846 | 4 44 | 7 28 | 11 46 | 4 49 | 7 23 | 11 52 | 4 53 | 7 18 | 11 58 | 5 8 | 7 4 | morn. |
| 25 | M | | 4 45 | 7 27 | morn. | 4 49 | 7 22 | morn. | 4 54 | 7 17 | morn. | 5 8 | 7 3 | 0 17 |
| 26 | Tu | St. Anne | 4 46 | 7 26 | 0 33 | 4 50 | 7 22 | 0 40 | 4 55 | 7 16 | 0 47 | 5 9 | 7 3 | 1 8 |
| 27 | W | | 4 47 | 7 25 | 1 37 | 4 51 | 7 21 | 1 44 | 4 56 | 7 15 | 1 51 | 5 10 | 7 2 | 2 12 |
| 28 | Th | Holy See applies to Congress, 1783 | 4 48 | 7 24 | 2 51 | 4 52 | 7 20 | 2 57 | 4 56 | 7 14 | 3 4 | 5 11 | 7 1 | 3 23 |
| 29 | Fr | St. Vincent's Abbey erected, 1855 | 4 49 | 7 23 | sets. | 4 53 | 7 19 | sets. | 4 57 | 7 14 | sets. | 5 11 | 7 0 | sets. |
| 30 | Sa | | 4 50 | 7 22 | 7 46 | 4 54 | 7 18 | 7 43 | 4 58 | 7 14 | 7 40 | 5 12 | 7 0 | 7 31 |
| 31 | S | | 4 51 | 7 21 | 8 28 | 4 55 | 7 17 | 8 27 | 4 59 | 7 13 | 8 25 | 5 13 | 6 59 | 8 20 |

| D. M. | DAY OF WEEK. | COLOR. | PROPER OF THE UNITED STATES. |
|---|---|---|---|
| 1 | Mond | W | St. Peter's Chains, gr. doub. 9th less. and com. of SS. after St. Paul, in L. and M. Gl. Cr. Pref. of App. In Vesp. com. of St. Paul, fol. and Sund. and St. Steph. |
| 2 | Tues | W | St. Alphonsus, B. C. doub. 9th less. of St. com. of St. in L. and M. Gl. in Vesp. com. of fol. |
| 3 | Wed | R | Find. of St. Stephen's Relics, semid. 2d coll. A Cunctis, 3d ad lib. Gl. Vesp. of fol. (hymn ch.) com. of prec. |
| 4 | Thurs | W | St. Dominic, C. doub. Gl. Vesp. of fol. com. of prec. |
| 5 | Frid | W | Dedicat. of St. Mary Majors, gr. doub. Gl. Cr. Pref. Et te in festiv. Vesp. of fol. com. of prec. and SS. Xystus, &c. Abstinence. |
| 6 | Satur | W | Transfig. of Our Lord, gr. doub. 9th less. and com. of SS. in L. and M. Gl. Cr. Pref. of Nativ. In Vesp. com. of fol. com. Sund. and St. Donatus. |
| 7 | SUND | W | Eighth Sund. after Pent. St. Cajetan, C. doub. 9th less. of Sund. com. of Sund. in L. and M. Last Gosp. of Sund. In Vesp. com. of Sund. and fol. |
| 8 | Mond | R | SS. Cyriacus and Comp. MM. Semid. 2d col. A Cunctis, 3d ad lib. In Vesp. of com. of St. Romanus. |
| 9 | Tues | R | Vigil 7 Brothers MM. (July 10), semid. 9th less. of Vigil, com. of Vig. in L. and M. 3d coll. A Cunctis. Last Gosp. of Vigil. Vesp. of fol. com. of prec. |
| 10 | Wed | R | St. Laurence, M. doub. 2 cl. with Oct. Gl. In Vesp. com. of fol. and SS. Tiburt. &c. |
| 11 | Thurs | W | St. Alexis, C. (July 17) semid. 9th less. of SS. com. of SS. and Oct. in L. and M. Vesp. of fol. com. of prec. and Oct. |
| 12 | Frid | W | St. Clare, V. doub. com. of Oct. in L. and M. Gl. In Vesp. com. of Oct. and SS. Hipp. &c. Abstinence. |
| 13 | Satur | R | Vigil (fast) of the Oct. semid. 9th less. of Vigil, com. of Vigil and SS. in L. and M. Vesp. from ch. of fol. Sund. com. of Oct. and St. Eusebius, C. |
| 14 | SUND | R | Ninth Sund. after Pent. (3d of August) com. of Oct. and St. Eusebius, in L. and M. Vesp. of fol. |
| 15 | Mond | † W | ASSUMPTION OF B. V. MARY, doub. 1st cl. with Oct. Gl. Cr. pref. Et te in Assumpt. In Vesp. com. only of fol. |
| 16 | Tues | † W | St. Hyacinth, C. doub. com. of Oct. of Assumpt. and St. Lawr. in L. and M. Gl. Cr. pref. of As. In Vesp. from ch. of fol. com. of prec. and Oct. |
| 17 | Wed | † R | Octave of St. Lawrence, doub. com. of Assumpt. in L. and M. Gl. &c. as yest. In Vesp. com. of Oct. of Assumpt. and St. Agapitus, M. |
| 18 | Thurs | † W | Of the Octave of Assumpt. semid. as on feast, 9th less. of St. com. of St. in L. and M. 3d coll. De Spir. San. |
| 19 | Frid | † W | Of the Octave as yest. in Mis. 2d coll. De Spir. San. 3d coll. De Ecc. or pro Papa. Vesp. of fol. com. of Oct. Abstinence. |
| 20 | Satur | † W | St. Bernard, Ab. and Doct. doub. and com. of Oct. in L. and M. (In medio, Epist. Justus.) Gl. &c. Vesp. of fol. com. of prec. and Sund. and Oct. |
| 21 | SUND | † W | Tenth Sund. after Pent. (4th of Aug.) St. Joachim, C. gr. doub. (hymn ch.) Less. 1, Noct. Beatus vir, 9th less. and com. of Sund. and Oct. in L. and M. Gl. &c. and last Gosp. of Sund. In Vesp. com. of Oct. Sund. and St. Timothy and Comp. |
| 22 | Mond | † W | Octave of Assumpt. as in prop. doub. 9th less. of St. com. of SS. in L. and M. Vesp. of Oct. com. of St. Philip. |
| 23 | Tues | W | St. Philip Beniti, C. doub. 1st Noct. incipit. Sund. prec. 9th less. of Vigil, com. of Vigil, in L. and M. Gl. last Gosp. of Vigil. Vesp. of fol. com. of prec. |
| 24 | Wed | R | St. Bartholomew, Ap. doub. 9th cl. Gl. Cr. Pref. of App. In Vesp. com. of fol. |
| 25 | Thurs | W | St. Lewis, King, C. semid. 2d col. A Cunctis, 3d ad lib. Gl. Vesp. of fol. com. of prec. and St. Zephyrinus, P. and M. |
| 26 | Frid | W | St. Jane Frances de Chantal, W. (from 21) doub. 9th less. of St. com. of St. in L. and M. Gl. Vesp. from ch. of fol. com. of prec. Abstinence. |
| 27 | Satur | W | St. Jos. Calasanc, C. doub. Gl. Vesp. from ch. of fol. com. of prec. Sund. and St. Hermes. |
| 28 | SUND | W | Eleventh Sund. after Pent. (5th of Aug.) St. Augustine, Bp. and D. doub. in prop. 9th less. of Sund. and com. of Sund. and St. in L. and M. Last Gosp. of Sund. Vesp. of fol. com. of prec. and Sund. and St. Sabina. |
| 29 | Mond | R | Beheading of St. John Bapt. gr. doub. 9th less. and com. of St. in L. and M. Gl. In Vesp. com. of fol. and Sund. and SS. Felix, &c. |
| 30 | Tues | W | St. Rosa of Lima, V. doub. 9th less. of St. in L. and M. Vesp. from ch. of fol. com. of prec. |
| 31 | Wed | W | St. Raymond, Non. C. doub. Gl. In Vesp. com. of fol. and the 12 Brothers MM. |

| 8th Month. | AUGUST, 1859. | 31 Days. |
|---|---|---|

## MOON'S PHASES.

| MOON'S PHASES. | | BOSTON. | NEW YORK. | BALTIMORE. | CHARLESTON. |
|---|---|---|---|---|---|
| | | H. M. | H. M. | H. M. | H. M. |
| First Quarter | 5th | 10 38 mo. | 10 26 mo. | 10 16 mo. | 10 2 mo. |
| Full Moon | 13th | 11 52 mo. | 11 40 mo. | 11 30 mo. | 11 16 mo. |
| Third Quarter | 21st | 9 2 mo. | 8 50 mo. | 8 40 mo. | 8 27 mo. |
| New Moon | 27th | 11 42 ev. | 11 30 ev. | 11 20 ev. | 11 6 ev. |

| Day of Month. | Day of Week. | ANNIVERSARIES, &c. |
|---|---|---|
| 1 | M | Ursulines and Hospital nuns land at Quebec. |
| 2 | Tu | |
| 3 | W | |
| 4 | Th | |
| 5 | Fr | Battle of Oriskany, 1777 |
| 6 | Sa | Atlantic Cable laid, 1858. |
| 7 | Su | |
| 8 | M | |
| 9 | Tu | |
| 10 | W | Ursuline Convent, Charlestown, burnt, 1834. |
| 11 | Th | |
| 12 | Fr | Mexico taken, 1591. |
| 13 | Sa | |
| 14 | Su | |
| 15 | M | Consecration of Bishop Carroll, 1790. |
| 16 | Tu | Battle of Bennington, 1777. Camden, 1780. |
| 17 | W | |
| 18 | Th | Santa Fé occupied, 1846. |
| 19 | Fr | |
| 20 | Sa | |
| 21 | Su | |
| 22 | M | |
| 23 | Tu | Father Rale killed, 1724. |
| 24 | W | Massacre of Lachine, 1689. |
| 25 | Th | |
| 26 | Fr | |
| 27 | Sa | Battle of Long Island, 1776 |
| 28 | Su | Synod of New York, 1842. |
| 29 | M | |
| 30 | Tu | |
| 31 | W | |

| D. M. | DAY OF WEEK. | COLOR. | PROPER OF THE UNITED STATES. |
|---|---|---|---|
| 1 | Thurs | W | St. Giles, Ab. simp. com. of SS. in L. 2d coll. *Fidelium*, 3d of SS. Gl. Vesp. of fol. (hymn ch.) |
| 2 | Frid | W | St. Stephen, C. semid. 2d coll. *A Cunctis*, 3d *ad lib.* Gl. Vesp. from ch. of fol. com. of prec. *Abstinence.* |
| 3 | Satur | W | Office of Immac. Concep. of B. V. M. semid. 2d col. *De Spir. San.* 3d *Ecc.* or *pro Papa.* Vesp. from ch. of fol. |
| 4 | SUND | G | Twelfth Sund. after Pent. (1st Sept.) 2 coll. *A Cunctis*, 3d coll. *ad lib.* Vesp. from ch. of fol. com. of Sund. |
| 5 | Mond | W | St. Lawrence Justinian, B. C. semid. coll. as yest. Vesp. of same. |
| 6 | Tues | G | Feria. Vesp. of Feria. |
| 7 | Wed | G | Feria. Vesp. of fol. |
| 8 | Thurs | † W | Nativity of B. V. Mary, doub. of the 2d cl. with Oct. 9th less. and com. of St. Adrian, in L. and M. Gl. Cr. Pref. *Et te in Nativ.* - In Vesp. com. of St. Gorgonius. |
| 9 | Frid | † W | Of the Oct. semid. 9th less, and com. of St. in L. and M. 3d coll. *De Spir. San.* Gl. Cr. &c. as yest. Vesp. of fol. com. of Oct. *Abstinence.* |
| 10 | Satur | † W | St. Nicholas Tolent. C. doub. com. of Oct. in L. and M. Gl. &c. as yest. In Vesp. com. of Oct. and Sund. and St. Protus and Comp.* |
| 11 | SUND | † W | 13th Sund. after Pent. (2d Sept.) Holy Name of Mary, gr. doub. 9th less. and com. of Sund. in L. and M. Gl. Cr. Pref. *Et te in festiv.* and last Gosp. of Sund. In Vesp. com. of Sund. |
| 12 | Mond | † W | Of the Oct. semid, 2d coll. *De Spir. San. Ecc.* or *pro Papa.* Gl. &c. Vesp. of same. |
| 13 | Tues | † W | Of Octave as yest. Vesp. of fol. com. of Oct. |
| 14 | Wed | † R | Exaltation of the Holy Cross, gr. doub. com. of Oct. in L. and M. Gl. Cr. Pref. *de Cruce.* In Vesp. com. of Oct. and St. Nicomedes. |
| 15 | Thurs | † W | Octave of Nativ. of B. V. Mary, doub. 9th less. and com. of St. in L. and M. Gl. Cr. In Vesp. com. of fol. and SS. Euphemia, &c. |
| 16 | Frid | R | SS. Cornelius and Cyprian, P. and M. semid. 9th less. of St. com. of St. in L. and M. 3 coll. *A Cunctis.* Vesp. of fol. (hymn ch.) com. of prec. *Abstinence.§* |
| 17 | Satur | W | Stigmata of St. Francis, C. doub. Gl. Vesp. from ch. of fol. com. of prec. |
| 18 | SUND | W | Fourteenth Sund. after Pent. (3 Sept.) Seven Dolors of B. V. Mary, gr. doub. 9th less. and com. of Sund. in L. and M. Gl. Cr. Pref. *Et te in Transfix.* and last Gosp. of Sund. Vesp. com. of fol. |
| 19 | Mond | R | St. Januarius and Comp. MM. doub. 1st Noct. *Incipit* of Sund. in prop. Vesp. |
| 20 | Tues | R | Vigil of St. Eustachius and Comp. MM. doub. 9th less. of Vigil, com. of Vigil in L. and M. Gl. last Gosp. of Vigil. Vesp. of fol. com. of prec. |
| 21 | Wed | P | Ember Day, fast, doub. 2d cl. 9th less. of Ember D. com. of Ember D. in L. and M. Gl. Cr. Pref. of ap. last Gosp. of Ember D. In Vesp. com. of fol. and St. Maurice and Comp. |
| 22 | Thurs | W | St. Thomas of Villanova, B. C. doub. (hymn, ch.) 9th less. and com. of SS. in L. and M. Gl. In Vesp. com. of fol. and St. Thecla. |
| 23 | Frid | R | Ember Day, fast, St. Linus, P. and M. semid. 1st Noct. *a Mileto*, 9th less. of Ember D. com. of Ember D. in L. and M. last Gosp. of Feria. Vesp. of fol. |
| 24 | Satur | W | Ember Day, fast, Our Lady of Mercy. gr. doub. 9th less. of Ember D. Gl. Cr. *Et te in Festiv.* com. of Ember D. in L. and M. last Gosp. of Ember D. Vesp. in com. of Sund. |
| 25 | SUND | G | Fifteenth Sund. after Pent. (4th Sept.) semid. 2d coll. *A Cunctis*, 3d *ad lib.* Vesp. of fol. com. of prec. and St. Cyprian and Comp. |
| 26 | Mond | W | St. Joseph a Cupertino (17th Sept.) C. doub. 9th less. of SS. com. of SS. in L. and M. In Vesp. com. of fol. |
| 27 | Tues | R | SS. Cosmas and Damian, MM. semid. 2d coll. *A Cunctis*, 3d *ad lib.* Vesp. from ch. of fol. |
| 28 | Wed | R | St. Wenceslaus, M. semid. Coll. as yest. Gl. Vesp. of fol. |
| 29 | Thurs | W | Dedication of St. Michael, Archang. doub. 2d cl. Gl. Cr. In Vesp. com. of fol. |
| 30 | Frid | W | St. Jerome, C. D. in prop. Gl. Cr. In Vesp. com. of fol. *Abstinence.* |

\* Consecration of Bishop of Louisville.
§    Do.      do.      Nashville.

# 9th Month.   SEPTEMBER, 1859.   30 Days.

| MOON'S PHASES. | BOSTON. | NEW YORK. | BALTIMORE. | CHARLESTON. |
|---|---|---|---|---|
| | H. M. | H. M. | H. M. | H. M. |
| First Quarter ...... 8d | 11 21 ev. | 11 9 ev. | 10 59 ev. | 10 45 ev. |
| Full Moon ......... 12th | 8 47 mo. | 8 35 mo. | 8 25 mo. | 8 12 mo. |
| Third Quarter ...... 19th | 5 30 ev. | 5 18 ev. | 5 8 ev. | 4 55 ev. |
| New Moon ........ 26th | 9 12 mo. | 9 0 mo. | 8 50 mo. | 8 37 mo. |

ANNIVERSARIES, &c.

1 Th  First Congress, 1774
2 Fr  Peace of Paris, 1788
3 Sa  Hudson discovers New York Bay, 1609
4 M
5 M
6 Tu
7 W
8 Th  St. Augustine founded, 1565
9 Fr  Battle of Lake Erie, 1818
10 Sa
11 S
12 M  Wolfe's victory over Montcalm, 1759
13 Tu
14 W  Slavery abolished in Mexico, 1829
15 Th
16 Fr
17 S  Constitution of the U. S. adopted, 1787
18 S
19 M  Battle of Stillwater, 1777
20 Tu
21 W
22 Th  Battle of Monterey, 1846
23 Fr
24 Sa
25 S
26 M
27 W
28 W  Michaelmas.
29 Th
30 Fr

| D. M. | DAY OF WEEK. | COLOR. | PROPER OF THE UNITED STATES. |
|---|---|---|---|
| 1 | Satur | † W | St. Remigius, B. C. semid. *ad lib.* or simp. *de precepto*, 1st Noct. *Incipit*, 5th Sund. Sept. (hymn ch.) 2d coll. *A Cunctis*, 3d *ad lib.* Gl. Vesp. of fol. com. of Sund. |
| 2 | SUND | † W | Sixteenth after Pent. (1st Oct.) Solemn. of the Holy Rosary, gr. doub. 9th less. and com. of Sund. in L. and M. Gl. Cr. Pref. *Et te in Solemnit.* and last Gosp. of Sund. In Vesp. com. of fol. and Sund. |
| 3 | Mond | † W | The Guardian Angels, doub. Gl. Cr. In Vesp. com. of fol. |
| 4 | Tues | † W | St. Francis, C. doub. 1st Noct. *ut Justus.* In Vesp. com. of fol. |
| 5 | Wed | † R | St. Placidus and Comp. MM. 1st and 2d less. of Sund. 1st simp. 2d coll. *Fidelium*, 3d coll. *A cunctis.* Vesp. of fol. |
| 6 | Thurs | † W | St. Bruno, C. doub. Gl. In Vesp. com. of fol. and SS. Sergius, &c. |
| 7 | Frid | W | St. Mark. P. C. simp. com. of SS. in L. 2d coll. *Fidelium*, 3d of SS. Gl. Vesp. of fol. *Abstinence.* |
| 8 | Satur | W | St. Bridget, Wid. doub. Gl. In Vesp. com of Sund. |
| 9 | SUND | G | Seventeenth Sunday after Pent. (2d Oct.) as in psal. and prop. In Vesp. com. of fol. |
| 10 | Mond | W | St. Francis Borgia, C. semid. coll. as yest. Gl. Vesp. from ch. of fol. com. of prec.* |
| 11 | Tues | R | SS. Dionysius and Comp. MM. semid. Coll. as 1st inst. Gl. Vesp. of same. |
| 12 | Wed | G | Feria. 2d coll. *Fidelium*, 3d *A Cunctis.* Vesp. of fol. (hymn ch.) |
| 13 | Thurs | W | St. Edward, C. semid. coll. as 1st inst. Vesp. of fol. com. of prec. ‡ |
| 14 | Frid | R | St. Callistus, P. M. doub. Gl. Vesp. from ch. of fol. com. of prec. *Abst.* |
| 15 | Satur | W | St. Theresa, V. doub. Gl. Vesp. of fol. com of prec. and Sund. |
| 16 | SUND | W | Eighteenth Sunday after Pent. (3d Oct.) Maternity of B. V. M. gr. doub. as in prop. 9th less. of Sund. com. of Sund. in L. and M. Pref. of B. M. *Et te in Festivitate*, last Gosp. of Sund. In Vesp. com. of Sund. and fol. |
| 17 | Mond | W | St. Hedwigis, Wid. semid. coll. as 1st. Gl. Vesp of fol. |
| 18 | Tues | R | St. Luke, Evan. doub. 2d cl. Gl. Cr. Pref. of App. In Vesp. com. of fol. |
| 19 | Wed | W | St. Peter of Alcantara, C. doub. (hymn ch.) Gl. Vesp. from ch. of fol. com. of prec. |
| 20 | Thurs | W | St. John Cantius, C. doub. Gl. Vesp. com. of St. Hilarion and SS. Ursula, &c., MM. |
| 21 | Frid | W | St. Hilarion, Ab. simp. com. of St. Ursula and Comp. in L. and M. 3d coll. *A Cunctis.* Vesp. of fol. *Abstinence.* |
| 22 | Satur | W | Office of Immaculate Conception, semid. as on feast and in prop. 2d coll. *De Spir. Sant.* 3d *Eccl.* or *pro Papa*, Pref. B. V. M. Vesp. from. ch. of Sund. com. of prec. |
| 23 | SUND | G | Nineteenth Sunday after Pent. (4th Oct.), semid. Vesp. of fol. com. of Sund. |
| 24 | Mond | W | St. Raphael, Archang., gr. doub. Gl. Cr. In Vesp. com. of SS. Crysanthus and Daria. |
| 25 | Tues | R | SS. Crysanthus and Daria, MM. simp. Gl. 2d or *A Cunctis*, 3d *ad lib.* Vesp. from ch. of fol. |
| 26 | Wed | R | St. Evaristus, P. M. simp. as yest. Gl. Vesp. of feria. |
| 27 | Thurs | P | Vigil of SS. Simon and Jude, 2d coll. *Concede*, 3d *Eccl.* or *pro Papa.* Vesp. of fol. |
| 28 | Frid | R | SS. Simon and Jude, App. doub. 2d cl. Gl. Cr. Pref. of App. In Vesp. com. of fol. *Abstinence.* * |
| 29 | Satur | W | Office of Immaculate Conception of B. V. M., semid. as on feast and in prop. 2d coll. *De Spir. Sanc.* 3d *Eccl.* or *pro Papa.* Vesp. from ch. of fol. com. of prec. |
| 30 | SUND | G | Twentieth after Pent. (1st Nov.), semid. as in psalt. and prop. 2d coll. *A Cunctis*, 3d *ad lib.* Vesp. of same.§ |
| 31 | Mond | P | Vigil (fast), as in psalt. and prop. 2d coll. *Fidelium*, 3d *De Spiritus Sanctus.* Vesp. of fol. |

* Consecration of Bishop of Cleveland.
‡ Do.     Abp. of Cincinnati.
§ Do.     Bps. of Brooklyn, Burlington, Newark.

| 10th Month. | OCTOBER, 1859. | | 31 Days. |
|---|---|---|---|

| MOON'S PHASES. | BOSTON. | NEW YORK. | BALTIMORE. | CHARLESTON. |
|---|---|---|---|---|
| | H. M. | H. M. | H. M. | H. M. |
| First Quarter ...... 3d | 3 48 ev. | 3 36 ev. | 3 26 ev. | 3 13 ev. |
| Full Moon ......... 11th | 7 8 ev. | 6 56 ev. | 6 46 ev. | 6 32 ev. |
| Third Quarter ...... 19th | 0 59 mo. | 0 47 mo. | 0 37 mo. | 0 23 mo. |
| New Moon ........ 25th | 7 49 ev. | 7 37 ev. | 7 27 ev. | 7 14 ev. |

The main body of the page consists of a dense astronomical calendar table giving Sun rises, Sun sets, and Moon sets for four regional groupings — BOSTON; NEW ENGLAND, N.Y. STATE, MICHI'N, WISCONSIN, IOWA, & OREGON / N. YORK CITY; PHILA., CONN., N. JER., PENN., OHIO, INDIANA, AND ILLINOIS / WASHINGTON; MARYL'ND, VIR-GINIA, KENT'KY, MISSOURI, AND CALIFORNIA / CHARLESTON; CAROL'A, TENN., GEORGIA, ALA., MISSISSIPPI, AND LOUISIANA — alongside the Day of Month, Day of Week, and ANNIVERSARIES columns.

**ANNIVERSARIES, &c.** (with Day of Week / Day of Month)

| Day of Week | Day of Month | Anniversary |
|---|---|---|
| Sa | 1 | Provincial Council, New York, 1854. |
| 8 | 2 | |
| M | 3 | First Council of Baltimore, 1829. |
| Tu | 4 | |
| W | 5 | |
| Th | 6 | |
| Fr | 7 | |
| Sa | 8 | |
| 8 | 9 | Columbus discovers America, 1492. |
| M | 10 | |
| Tu | 11 | |
| W | 12 | First Carmelite Conv. founded in U. S., 1790. |
| Th | 13 | |
| Fr | 14 | |
| Sa | 15 | |
| 8 | 16 | Dongan convenes first N. Y. Assembly, 1638. |
| M | 17 | Father Jogues killed, 1646. |
| Tu | 18 | Battle of Yorktown, 1781. |
| W | 19 | Second Council of Baltimore, 1833. |
| Th | 20 | |
| Fr | 21 | |
| Sa | 22 | Philadelphia settled, 1682. |
| 8 | 23 | |
| M | 24 | |
| Tu | 25 | Battle of White Plains, 1776. |
| W | 26 | School debate, New York, 1840. |
| Th | 27 | New York Charter of Liberties, 1683. |
| Fr | 28 | All-Hallow Eve. |
| Sa | 29 | |
| 8 | 30 | |
| M | 31 | |

| D. M. | DAY OF WEEK. | COLOR. | PROPER OF THE UNITED STATES. |
|---|---|---|---|
| 1 | Tues | W | ALL SAINTS, doub. 1st cl. with Oct. after *Bened. Dom.* are recited Vesp. *De-functor.* and then *Complin.** |
| 2 | Wed | B | Commemoration of All Souls. Office of the Oct. semid. Less. 1st Noct. from prec. Sund. At Lauds after *Bened. Dom.* are recited Matins and Lauds *Defunctor.* Vesp. of the Oct. |
| 3 | Thurs | W | Of the Octave semid. 2d coll. *De Spir. San.* 3d *Eccl.* or *pro Papa.* Gl. Cr. Vesp. of fol. com. of Oct. and SS. Vital, &c. |
| 4 | Frid | W | St. Charles Borromeo, B. C. doub. 9th less. and com. of SS. (after Oct.) in L. and M. Gl. Cr. In Vesp. com. of Oct. *Abstinence.* |
| 5 | Satur | W | Of the Octave, semid. as on 3d inst. Gl. Cr. Vesp. from ch. of fol. com. of Oct.‡ |
| 6 | SUND | W | Twenty-first Sund. after Pent. (2d Nov.) semid. as in prop. and psal. com. of Oct. in L. and M. Vesp. com. of fol. |
| 7 | Mond | W | Of the Octave, semid. as 3d inst. Vesp. of fol. com. of SS. 4 Martyrs. |
| 8 | Tues | W | Octave of All Saints, doub. as in feast and in prop 9th less. of SS. com. of SS. in L. and M. Vesp. from ch. of fol. com. of Oct. and St. Theodore. |
| 9 | Wed | W | Dedication of St. Savior's doub. 9th less. and com. of St. in L. and M. Gl. Cr. Vesp. from ch. of fol. com. of prec. and SS. Tryphon, &c. |
| 10 | Thurs | W | St. Andrew Avellino, C. doub. 9th less. and com. of SS. in L. and M. Gl. Vesp. from ch. of fol. com. of prec. and St. Menna.§ |
| 11 | Frid | W | St. Martin, B. C. doub. Less. 1 Noct. *Fidelis sermo,* 9th less. and com. of St. in L. and M. Gl. In Vesp. com. of fol. *Abstinence.* |
| 12 | Satur | R | St. Martin, P. M. semid. 2d coll. *A Cunctis,* 3d *ad lib.* Gl. Vesp. of fol. com. of Sund. and prec. |
| 13 | SUND | W | Twenty-second Sund. after Pent. (3d Nov.) feast of the Patronage of the B. V. Mary, gr. doub. 9th less. of Sund. com. of Sund. in L. and M. Gl. Cr. pref. B. M. *Et te in Festiv.* In Vesp. com. of fol. and Sund. |
| 14 | Mond | W | St. Stanislaus Kostka, C. doub. Gl. Vesp. from ch. of fol. com. of prec. |
| 15 | Tues | W | St. Gertrude, V. doub. *Incipit* Joel, 1st Noct. In Vesp. com. fol. |
| 16 | Wed | W | St. Didacus, C. semid. coll. as yest. Gl. Vesp. from ch. of fol. com. of prec. |
| 17 | Thurs | W | St. Gregory Thaumat. B. C. semid. 1st Noct. *Incipit* Amos, coll. as 12th inst. Gl. Vesp. of fol. com. of prec. |
| 18 | Frid | W | Dedicat. of SS. Peter and Paul, gr. doub. 5th and 6th less. as recently altered, Gl. Cr. Vesp. from ch. of fol. com. of prec. and St. Pontianus. *Abst.* |
| 19 | Satur | W | St. Elizabeth, W. d 1st Noct. 1st less. *Incipit* Abdias, 2d and 3d less. *Incipit* Jonas, 9th less. and com. of St. in L. and M. Gl. Vesp. from ch. of fol. (hymn cliff) com. of prec. and Sund. |
| 20 | SUND | G | Twenty-fourth Sund. after Pent. (4th Nov.) St. Felix a Valois, C. doub. 9th less. of Sund. (last) in L. and M. Gl. Cr. last Gosp. of Sund. Vesp. of fol. com. of prec. and Sund. |
| 21 | Mond | W | Presentation of B. V. Mary, gr. doub. Gl. Cr. Pref. *Et te in Presentat.* In Vesp. com. of fol.** |
| 22 | Tues | R | St. Cecilia, V. M. doub. 1st less. *De Virginibus.* Vesp. from ch. of fol. com. of prec. |
| 23 | Wed | R | St. Clement, P. M. doub. less. 1 Noct. *A Mileto,* 9th less. and com. of St. in L. and M. Gl. Vesp. from ch. of fol. (hymn ch.) com. of prec. and St. ‡‡ |
| 24 | Thurs | W | St. John of the Cross, C. d. 1st less. *Incipit* Nahum, 2d *Incipit* Abacuc, 3d *Incipit* Sophonias, 9th less. and com. of St. in L. and M. Gl. Vesp. from ch. of fol. com. of prec. |
| 25 | Frid | R | St. Catharine, V. and M. doub. 1st Noct. 1st less. *Incipit* Aggæus, 2d and 3d *Incipit* Zacharias. In Vesp. com. of fol. and St. Peter, M. *Abst.* |
| 26 | Satur | W | Office of Immac. Concep. 1st Noct. less. *Incipit* Malachias, 9th less. of St. com. of St. in L. and M. 3d coll. *De Spir. San.* pref. B. M. Vesp. from ch. of fol. |
| 27 | SUND | P | First Sund. in Advent, semid. as in psal. and prop. Vesp. of same. |
| 28 | Mond | P | Feria, as in psal. and prop. com. of St. Saturninus, M. Vesp. of same. |
| 29 | Tues | P | Feria, as yest. com. of St. Saturninus in L. and M. Mass of Vigil, com. of festiv. and St. Saturninus. Vesp. of fol. com. of feria. |
| 30 | Wed | R | St. Andrew, Ap. doub. 2d cl. com. of feria. in L. and M. Gl. Cr. Pref. of App. In Vesp. com. of feria.§§ |

\* Consecration of Bishop of Sant St. Mary's and Covington.
‡ Do..   do.   Mobile.
§ Do.   do.   Richmond.
** Do.   Abp. of New Orleans.
‡‡ Do.   Bishop of Santa Fé.
§§ Do.   Abp. of St. Louis.

## 11th Month.     NOVEMBER, 1859.     30 Days.

| MOON'S PHASES. | | BOSTON. | NEW YORK. | BALTIMORE. | CHARLESTON. |
|---|---|---|---|---|---|
| | | H. M. | H. M. | H. M. | H. M. |
| First Quarter | 2d | 11 34 mo. | 11 22 mo. | 11 12 mo. | 10 59 mo. |
| Full Moon | 10th | 9 21 mo. | 9 9 mo. | 8 59 mo. | 8 46 mo. |
| Third Quarter | 17th | 8 23 mo. | 8 11 mo. | 8 1 mo. | 7 47 mo. |
| New Moon | 24th | 8 59 mo. | 8 47 mo. | 8 37 mo. | 8 24 mo. |

*(The remainder of the page consists of rotated columnar tables giving Sun rises, Sun sets, and Moon sets/rises for the regions: CHARLESTON, N., CAROLINA, TENN., GEORGIA, ALA., MISSISSIPPI, AND LOUISIANA; WASHINGTON, MARYLAND, VIRGINIA, KENTUCKY, MISSOURI, AND CALIFORNIA; N. YORK CITY, PHILADELPHIA, CONN., N. JERSEY, PENN., OHIO, INDIANA, AND ILLINOIS; BOSTON, NEW ENGLAND, N.Y. STATE, MICHIGAN, WISCONSIN, IOWA, & OREGON; together with columns for Day of Week, Day of Month, and ANNIVERSARIES.)*

**ANNIVERSARIES, &c.**

1 Tu — All Saints
2 W — All Souls
3 Th — St. Malachy
4 Fr — Bp. Fisget cons., 1810
5 Sa
6 S
7 M
8 Tu — See of Baltimore founded, 1789
9 W — First Synod of Baltimore, 1791
10 Th
11 Fr
12 Sa
13 S
14 M — Charles Carroll died, 1839
15 Tu — Articles of Confederation adopted, 1777
16 W
17 Th
18 Fr — St. Mary's Chapel, Ganentaa, N. Y., 1655
19 Sa — Treaty with England, 1794
20 S
21 M
22 Tu
23 W
24 Th — Peace with Great Britain, 1814
25 Fr — Cardinal Pole died, 1558
26 Sa
27 S — Castle of Ulloa taken, 1838
28 M
29 Tu
30 W

2

| D. M. | DAY OF WEEK. | COLOR. | PROPER OF THE UNITED STATES. |
|---|---|---|---|
| 1 | Thurs | P | Feria. 2d coll. *Deus qui*, 3d *Eccl.* or *pro Papa.* Vesp. of fol. com. of feria. |
| 2 | Frid | R | (Fast-day) St. Bibiana, V. M. semid. com. of feria in L. and M. 3d coll. *Deus qui.* Gl. Vesp. of fol. com. of prec. and feria. |
| 3 | Satur | W | St. Francis Xavier, C. doub. com. of feria in L. and M. Vesp. com. of Sund. and St. Barbara. |
| 4 | SUND | P | Second Sunday in Advent, semid. com. of St. Barbara in L. and M. 3d. coll. *de B. V. M.* Vesp. of fol. com. of Sund. and St. Sabba. |
| 5 | Mond | W | St. Peter Chrysologus, B. C. Doctor, double, less. 1st Noct. *Fidelis sermo*, com. of feria and St. in L. and M. Gl. Cr. Vesp. from ch. of fol. com. of prec. and feria. |
| 6 | Tues | W | St. Nicholas, B. C. doub. (6th inst.) (hymn ch.) com. of Oct. in feria in L. and M. Gl. Cr., &c. Vesp. from ch. of fol. com. of prec. and feria. |
| 7 | Wed | W | St. Ambrose, B. C. D. doub. less. 1st Noct. *Fidelis sermo*, com. of feria in L. and M. Gl. Cr. Vesp. of fol. com. of prec. and feria. |
| 8 | Thurs | † W | IMMAC. CONCEP. OF B. V. M., doub. 1st cl. with Oct. com. of feria in L. and M. Gl. Cr. Pref. *Et te in Concep. Im.* during the Oct. Vesp. com. of feria. |
| 9 | Frid | † W | (Fast-day) of the Oct. semid. com. of feria and St. in L. and M. Gl. Cr., &c. Vesp. of same, com. of feria and St. Melchias, P. and M. |
| 10 | Satur | † W | Of the Octave, com. of feria and St. in L. and M. Vesp. from ch. of Sund. com. of Oct. (*To-morrow, the altar is adorned with flowers.*) |
| 11 | SUND | † W | Third of Advent, semid. com. of Oct. in L. Mass of Concep. com. of Sund. Gl., &c., as oc. feast, and last Gosp. of Sund. Vesp. com. of fol. and Oct. |
| 12 | Mond | † W | St. Damasus, P. C. semid. com. of Oct. and feria in L. and M. Gl. Cr., &c. Vesp. of fol. com. of prec. and feria. |
| 13 | Tues | † R | St. Lucy, V. M. doub. (yest.) com. of Oct. and feria in L. and M. Gl. Cr., &c. Vesp. of fol. com. of prec. and feria. |
| 14 | Wed | † W | Ember day. Of Octave, semid. 9th less. of feria, com. of feria in L. and M. 2d of oct. 3d of *Spiritus Sanctus*, Pref. of B. V. M. last Gosp. of feria. Vesp. of fol. |
| 15 | Thurs | † W | Octave of Conception. doub. com. of feria in L. and M. Gl. Cr., &c. Vesp. com. of fol. and feria. |
| 16 | Frid | † R | Ember day (fast). St. Eusebius, B. M. semid. less. 1st Noct. *A Mileto*, 9th less. and com. of feria in L. and M. 3d coll. *Deus qui*, Gl. and last Gosp. of feria. In Vesp. com. of feria. |
| 17 | Satur | P | Ember day (fast), in L. and hours, Ant. *Propheta.* |
| 18 | SUND | P | Fourth Sunday of Advent, semid. as in psalt. and prop. Vesp. of fol. com. of Sund. *O Adonai.* |
| 19 | Mond | W | Expectation of Delivery of B. V. M., gr. doub. (yest.) as in prop. com. of feria in L. and M. (Ant. *Dicit Dom.*) Pref. of B. V. M. *Et te in Expectatione.* In Vesp. com. of feria, *O Radix.* |
| 20 | Tues | P | Vigil. Office of feria, Ant. *Rorate*, Bened. Ant. *Consurge*, Mass of Vigil, 2d coll. of feria, 3d. of B. V. M. Vesp. of fol. com. of feria, *O Clavis.* |
| 21 | Wed | R | St. Thomas, Ap. doub. 2d cl. com. of feria, *Nolite Timere* in L. and M. Gl. Cr. Pref. of App. In Vesp. com. of feria, Ant. *O Clavis.* |
| 22 | Thurs | P | Feria, at L. and hours, Ant. *de Sim. at Bened.* *Consolamini.* Vesp. of feria, Ant. *O Rex.* |
| 23 | Frid | P | Feria, as yest. and in prop. at L. Ant. *Constantes* at Bened. *Ecce Completa.* Vesp. of feria, Ant. at Mag. *O Emmanuel.* (Fast-day.) |
| 24 | Satur | P | Vigil of Nativ. of our Lord (fast-day), at L. and M. doub. coll. as in prop. Vesp. of fol. |
| 25 | SUND | † W | NATIVITY OF OUR LORD, or CHRISTMAS, doub. 1st cl. with Oct. all prop. Gl. Cr. Pref. and *Communic.* prop. during the Oct. Vesp. com. of St. Steph. |
| 26 | Mond | † R | St. Stephen, Protomartyr, doub. 2d cl. with Oct. com. of Oct. in L. and M. Gl. &c. Vesp. of Nativ. from ch. of St. Stephen, com. of fol. and Oct. |
| 27 | Tues | † P | St. John, Ap. and Evang. doub. 2d. cl. with Oct. com. of Nativ. and St. Steph. in L. and M. Gl. &c. Vesp. of Nativ. from ch. of St. John, com. of fol. and 2 Octs. |
| 28 | Wed | † P | The Holy Innocents, MM. doub. 2d cl. with Oct. com. of 3 Octs. in L. and M. Cr., &c. Vesp. of Nativ. from ch. of H. Innoc. com. of fol. and 3 Octaves. |
| 29 | Thurs | † R | St. Thomas of Canterbury, B. M. semid. less. 1st Noct. *A Mileto*, com. of 4 Octs. in L. and M. Gl., &c , as 27th inst. Vesp. semid. of Nativ. from ch. of Sund. in the Oct. of Nativ. com. of prec. and 4 Octaves. |
| 30 | Frid | † W | Of the Sund. within the Oct. semid. com. of 4 Octs. in L. and M. Gl., &c., as yest. Vesp. doub. of Nativ. from ch. of fol. com. of Sund. and 4 Octs. *Abstinence.* |
| 31 | Satur | † W | St. Silvester, P. C. doub. com. of 4 Octs. in L. and M. Gl., &c., as yest. Vesp. of Circumcis. |

# 12th Month.  DECEMBER, 1859.  31 Days.

| MOON'S PHASES. | BOSTON. | NEW YORK. | BALTIMORE. | CHARLESTON. |
|---|---|---|---|---|
| | H. M. | H. M. | H. M. | H. M. |
| First Quarter ...... 2d | 9 6 mo. | 8 54 mo. | 8 44 mo. | 8 80 mo. |
| Full Moon ......... 9th | 10 29 ev. | 10 17 ev. | 10 7 ev. | 9 54 ev. |
| Third Quarter...... 16th | 4 82 ev. | 4 20 ev. | 4 10 ev. | 8 57 ev. |
| New Moon ........ 24th | 1 3 mo. | 0 51 mo. | 0 41 mo. | 0 28 mo. |

| Day of Month. | Day of Week. | ANNIVERSARIES, &c. |
|---|---|---|
| 1 | Th | Council of Trent opens, 1545 |
| 2 | Fr | French Empire, 1852 |
| 3 | Su | Death of Archbishop Carroll, 1815 |
| 4 | S | |
| 5 | M | |
| 6 | Tu | |
| 7 | W | Patronal feast of the U. S. |
| 8 | Th | |
| 9 | Fr | |
| 10 | Sa | |
| 11 | S | Indiana admitted, 1816 |
| 12 | M | |
| 13 | Tu | |
| 14 | W | |
| 15 | Th | |
| 16 | Fr | Great fire in New York, 1885 |
| 17 | Sa | |
| 18 | S | |
| 19 | M | Bishop Dubois died, 1842 |
| 20 | Tu | |
| 21 | W | |
| 22 | Th | |
| 23 | Fr | Treaty of Ghent, 1814 |
| 24 | Sa | Christmas |
| 25 | S | |
| 26 | M | |
| 27 | Tu | |
| 28 | W | Texas admitted, 1845 |
| 29 | Th | |
| 30 | Fr | |
| 31 | Sa | |

# GOVERNMENT OF THE CHURCH.

## POPE.

His Holiness PIUS IX. (John Mary Mastai Ferretti), born at Sinigaglia,
May 13, 1792 ; elected Supreme Pontiff, June 16, 1846.

## CARDINAL BISHOPS.

MOST EMINENT.

DATE.

| | | |
|---|---|---|
| Vincent Macchi, Bishop of Ostea and Velletri........... | 2 Oct., | 1826. |
| Mario Mattei, Bishop of Porto and St. Rufina ........... | 2 July, | 1832. |
| Constantino Patrizi, Bishop of Albano.................. | 23 June, | 1834. |
| Louis Amat, Bishop of Palestrina ..................... | 19 May, | 1837. |
| Gabriel Ferretti, Bishop of Sabina..................... | 30 Nov., | 1838. |
| Anthony Cagiano de Azevedo, Bishop of Frascati........ | 22 Jan., | 1844. |

## CARDINAL PRIESTS.

| | | |
|---|---|---|
| Benedict Barbarini, of the title of San Lorenzo in Lucina. | 2 Oct., | 1826. |
| Hugh Peter Spinola, of the title of SS. Silvestro é Martino | 30 Sept., | 1831. |
| Adrian Freschi, of the title of St. Mary of Victory ....... | 23 June, | 1834. |
| Gabriel della Genga Sermattei, of the title of St. Jerome of the Slavonians............................... | 1 Feb., | 1836. |
| Chiarissimo Falconieri Mellini, of the title of San Marcello | 12 Feb., | 1838. |
| Philip de Angelis, of the title of St. Bernard, Apb. of Fermo | 13 Sept., | 1838. |
| Engelbert Sterckx, of the title of St. Bartholomew, Apb. of Mechlin........................................ | " | " |
| Gaspar Bernard Pianetti, of the title of St. Sixtus, Bishop of Viterbo....................................... | 23 Dec., | 1839. |
| Louis Vannicelli-Casoni, of the title of St. Praxedes, Apb. of Ferrara....................................... | " | " |
| Louis Altieri, of the title of St. Mary in Portico......... | 14 Dec., | 1840. |
| Louis James Maurice de Bonald, of the title of M. H. Trinity in Monte Pinc., Apb. of Lyons ...................... | 1 March, | 1841. |
| Frederick Joseph Schwartzenburg, of the title of St. Augustine, Abp. of Prague ........................., | 24 Jan., | 1842. |
| Cosimo Corsi, of the title of SS. John and Paul.......... | 24 Jan., | 1842. |
| Francis Paul Villadicani, of the title of St. Alexius, Apb. of Messina....................................... | 27 Jan., | 1843. |
| Fabius Mary Asquini, of the title of St. Stephen in the Monte Celio..................................... | 22 Jan., | 1844. |
| Nicholas Clarelli-Paracciani, of the title of St. Peter in Vinc...................................... | " | " |
| Dominic Carafa di Traetto, of the title of St. Mary of the Angels, Apb. of Benevento...................... | 22 July, | 1844. |
| James Piccolomini, of the title of St. Mark............. | " | " |
| Justus Riario Sforza, of the title of St. Sabina, Apb. of Naples | 19 Jan., | 1846. |
| Cajetan Baluffi, of the title of St. Peter and Marcellinus, Abp. of Imola.................................. | 21 Dec., | 1846. |
| James Mary Anthony Celestine du Pont, of the title of St. Mary del Popolo, Apb. of Bourges ................ | 12 Jan., | 1847. |
| James Mary Adrian Cæsarius Mathieu, of the title of St. Silvester, Apb. of Besançon..................... | 30 Sept., | 1850. |

CARDINALS. •

Thomas Gousset, of the title of St. Calixtus, Apb. of Rheims 30 Sept., 1850.
John Geissel, of the title of San Lorenzo Pane e Perna,
Apb. of Cologne.................................. " "
Nicholas Wiseman, of the title of St. Pudentiana, Apb. of
Westminster.................................... " "
Joseph Cosenza, of the title of St. Mary Transpont, Apb. of
Capua ....................................... " "
Dominic Lucciardi, of the title of St. Clement, Bishop of
Sinigaglia.................................... 15 M'ch, 1852.
Fred. Aug. Ferd. Donnet, of the title of St. Mary in Via,
Abp. of Bordeaux.............................. " "
Michael Viale-Prela, of the title of St. Andrew and St.
Gregory, Abp. of Bologna...................... " "
Jerome d'Andrea, of the title of St. Agnes extra m...... " "
Ch. Louis Morichini, of the title of St. Onofrio, Bp. of Jesi " "
John Brunelli, of the title of St. Cecilia, Abp. of Osimo
and Cingoli................................... " "
John Scitowski, of the title of Holy Cross in Jerusalem,
Abp. of Strigonia ............................. 7 March, 1853.
Francis Nich. Magd. Morlot, of the title of SS. Nereus and
Archilleus, Abp. of Paris...................... " "
Justus Recanati, Capucin, of the title of Twelve H. Apos-
tles.......................................... " "
Camillus di Pietro................................ 19 Dec., 1853.
Joachim Pecci, of the title of St. Chrysogonus, Bishop of
Perugia...................................... " "
Joseph Osmar Rauscher, Abp. of Vienna............. 19 Dec., 1855.
Charles de Reisach, of the title of St. Anastasia, Abp. of
Munich...................................... " "
Clement Villecourt, of the title of St. Pancras extra m... " • "
Francis Gaude, O.S.D., of the title of St. Mary sopra Minerva " "
Alex. Barnabo, of the title of St. Susanna, Prefect of the
Congregation de Propaganda fide ................ 16 June, 1856.
Cyril Alameda i Brea, Abp. of Toledo............... 15 Mch., 1858.○
Anthony Benedict Antonucci, Bp. of Ancona and Umane.. " "
Emmanuel Joachim Tarancon, of the title of
Abp. of Seville............................... " "
Henry Orfei, of the title of      Bp. of Cesena   " "
Joseph Milesi Pironi Ferretti ...................... " "

CARDINAL DEACONS.

Louis Gazzoli,    Deacon of St. Mary in via lata ........ 30 Sept., 1831.
Louis Ciacchi,    "    St. Angelo................. 12 Feb., 1838.
Joseph Ugolini,   "    St. Mary's in via lata ....... " "
Peter Marini,     "    St. Nicholas, in Carcere..... 21 Dec., 1846.
Joseph Bofondi,   "    St. Cæsarius ............... " "
James Antonelli,  "    St. Agatha in Suburra ....... 11 June, 1847.
Robert Roberti, • "    St. Mary in Dominica....... 30 Sept., 1850.
Dominic Savelli,  "    St. Mary in Aquiro ......... 7 March, 1853.
Prosper Caterini, "    St. Mary delle Scala........ " "
Vincent Santucci, "    St. Mary ad Martyres ....... " "
Gaspar Grasselini "    SS. Vitus and Modestus...... 16 June, 1856.
Peter de Silvestro "    ........ 15 M'ch, 1858.○
Theodulphus Mertel, "    ..... " "

* Proclaimed in Consistory.

# ECCLESIASTICAL DIVISION

OF THE

# UNITED STATES.

THE Catholic Church in the United States comprises seven Provinces, of which the Metropolitan Sees are New York, Baltimore, New Orleans, Cincinnati, St. Louis, San Francisco, and Oregon.

## PROVINCE OF NEW YORK.

The Province of New York comprises the Dioceses of New York, Portland, Burlington, Boston, Hartford, Brooklyn, Albany, Buffalo, and Newark, including the New England States, New York, and New Jersey.

## DIOCESE OF NEW YORK.

(NEO EBORACENSIS.)

*Erected in* 1808.

The Diocese of New York comprises the City and County of New York, Richmond, Westchester, Putnam, Dutchess, Rockland, Orange, Ulster, Delaware, and Sullivan counties, in the State of New York.

## ARCHBISHOP.

Most Rev. John Hughes, D.D. Consecrated January 7, 1838, Bishop of Basileopolis and Coadjutor to the Bishop of New York. Succeeded as Bishop in 1842—created Archbishop in 1850.

### PREDECESSORS.

Rt. Rev. Luke Concanen, O.S.D., 1st Bishop, cons. April 24, 1808, Died in 1810.
Rt. Rev. John Connolly, O.S.D., 2d Bishop, cons. 6th Nov., 1814, Died in 1825.
Rt. Rev. John Dubois, 3d Bishop, cons. 29th Oct. 1826. Died in 1842.

---

## DIOCESE OF PORTLAND.

### 1855.

Comprising the States of Maine and New Hampshire.

#### BISHOP.

Rt. Rev. David W. Bacon, D.D., 1st Bishop, consecrated April 22, 1855.

---

## DIOCESE OF BOSTON.

### 1808.

Comprising the State of Massachusetts.

#### BISHOP.

Rt. Rev. John B. Fitzpatrick, D.D., consecrated March 24, 1844.

##### PREDECESSORS.

Rt. Rev. John B. Cheverus, D.D., consecrated Nov. 1, 1810. Died Card. Abp. of Bordeaux in 1836.
Rt. Rev. Benedict Fenwick, D.D., consecrated in 1825. Died 1845.

---

## DIOCESE OF HARTFORD.

### 1844.

Comprising the States of Rhode Island and Connecticut.

#### BISHOP.

Rt. Rev. Francis P. M'Farland, D.D., consecrated February 14th, 1858.

Rt. Rev. WILLIAM TYLER, D.D., 1st Bishop, consecrated March 17, 1844. Died in 1849.
Rt. Rev. BERNARD O'REILLY, D.D., 2d Bishop, consecrated in 1850. Lost at sea in 1856.

# DIOCESE OF BROOKLYN.

## 1853.

Comprising Long Island in the State of New York.

### BISHOP.

Rt. Rev. JOHN LOUGHLIN, D.D., 1st Bishop, consecrated Oct. 30, 1853.

# DIOCESE OF ALBANY.

## 1847.

Comprising all New York, north of the 42nd degree of north latitude, and east of the western limit of Cayuga, Tompkins, and Tioga counties.

### BISHOP.

Right Rev. JOHN McCLOSKEY, D.D., 1st Bishop, consecrated Bishop of Axiern, and Coadjutor to the Bishop of New York, March 10, 1844; transferred to Albany in 1847.

# DIOCESE OF BUFFALO.

## 1847.

This Diocese comprises the Counties of Erie, Niagara, Orleans, Genesee, Monroe, Livingston, Ontario, Wayne, Cayuga, Chatauque, Wyoming, Cattaraugus, Steuben, Chemung, Tioga, Tompkins, Seneca, and Yates, in the State of New York.

### BISHOP.

Right Rev. JOHN TIMON, D.D., C.M., 1st Bishop, consecrated Oct. 17, 1847.

# DIOCESE OF NEWARK.

## 1853.

Comprising the State of New Jersey.

### BISHOP.

Right Rev. JAMES ROOSEVELT BAYLEY, D.D., 1st Bishop, consecrated Oct. 30, 1853.

# PROVINCE OF BALTIMORE.

Comprising the dioceses of Baltimore, Philadelphia, Pittsburg, Erie, Richmond, Wheeling, Charleston, and Savannah, with the Vicariate Apostolic of Florida, and extending over the District of Columbia, and the States of Maryland, Virginia, North and South Carolina, Georgia, and the eastern section of Florida.

## DIOCESE OF BALTIMORE.

Established 1789.

Comprising MARYLAND and the District of Columbia, as originally laid out.

### ARCHBISHOP.

Most Rev. FRANCIS PATRICK KENRICK, D.D., consecrated Bishop of Arath and coadjutor to the Bishop of Philadelphia, June 6, 1830, Bishop of Philadelphia in 1842, transferred to the See of Baltimore, August 19, 1851.

### PREDECESSORS.

Most Rev. JOHN CARROLL, D.D., consec. Aug. 15, 1790.  Died in 1815.
Most Rev. LEONARD NEALE, D.D., "          1800.       "   " 1817.
Most Rev. AMBROSE MARECHAL, D.D., cons. Dec. 14, 1817.   "   " 1828.
Most Rev. JAMES WHITFIELD, D.D.,  " May 25, 1828.       "   " 1834.
Most Rev. SAMUEL ECCLESTON, D.D.,    Sep. 14, 1834.     "   " 1851.

## DIOCESE OF PHILADELPHIA.

1809.

Comprising the State of Delaware and all that part of Pennsylvania lying east of the western limit of Tioga, Clinton, Centre, Mifflin, Juniata, Franklin, and Fulton Counties.

### BISHOPS.

Right Rev. JOHN NEPOMUCENE NEUMANN, D.D., C.SS.R., 4th Bishop, consecrated March 2, 1852.
Right Rev. JAMES F. WOOD, D.D., Bishop of Antigonia *in part;* and Coadjutor to the Bishop of Philadelphia, consecrated May 26, 1857.

*Predecessors.*

Right Rev. MICHAEL EGAN, D.D. (O.S.F.), consecrated Oct. 28, 1810; died 1814.
Right Rev. HENRY CONWELL, consecrated in 1820; died 1842.
Right Rev. FRANCIS F. KENRICK, D.D., consecrated June 6, 1830; transferred to Baltimore in 1851.

2*

# DIOCESE OF PITTSBURG.

## 1843.

Comprising Allegheny, Greene, Washington, Fayette, Beaver, Butler, Lawrence, Armstrong, Indiana, Westmoreland, Cambria, Blair, Huntingdon, Bedford, and Somerset Counties, in the State of Pennsylvania.

BISHOP.

Rt. Rev. MICHAEL O'CONNOR, D.D., 1st Bishop, consecrated August 15th, 1843, and transferred from Erie, Dec. 20th, 1853.

# DIOCESE OF ERIE.

## 1853.

Comprising Mercer, Venango, Clarion, Jefferson, Clearfield, Elk, McKean, and Potter Counties, and all that part of PENNSYLVANIA North and West of them.

BISHOP.

Rt. Rev. JOSUE M. YOUNG, D.D., 2d Bishop, consecrated April 23, 1854.

# DIOCESE OF RICHMOND.

## 1821.

Comprising that part of the State of VIRGINIA lying East of the Western limit of Hardy, Pendleton, Highland, Bath, Alleghany, Monroe, Giles, Montgomery, Franklin, and Patrick Counties.

BISHOP.

Rt. Rev. JOHN M'GILL, D.D., 3rd Bishop, consecrated Nov. 10, 1850.

PREDECESSOR.

Rt. Rev. PATRICK KELLY, D.D., 1st Bishop, consecrated in 1821; transferred the next year to Waterford and Lismore.

Rt. Rev. RICHARD V. WHELAN, D.D., 2d Bishop, consecrated March 21, 1841, transferred to Wheeling, July 23, 1850.

# DIOCESE OF WHEELING.

## 1850.

Comprising all that part of the State of VIRGINIA, West of the Eastern limit of the Counties of Hardy, Pendleton, Highland, Bath, Alleghany, Monroe, Giles, Montgomery, Franklin, and Patrick.

BISHOP.

Rt. Rev. RICHARD VINCENT WHELAN, D.D., 1st Bishop, transferred from Richmond, July 23, 1850.

# DIOCESE OF CHARLESTON.
## 1820.
### Comprising the States of North and South Carolina.

**BISHOP.**

Rt. Rev. P. N. LYNCH, D.D., consecrated Feb. 14, 1858.

**PREDECESSORS.**

Rt. Rev. JOHN ENGLAND, 1st Bishop, consecrated 21st Sept. 1820, died in 1842.
Rt. Rev. WILLIAM CLANCY, coadjutor, transferred to Guiana, died in 1847.
Rt. Rev. IGNATIUS A. REYNOLDS, D.D., 2d Bishop, consecrated 19th March, 1844, died in 1855.

---

# DIOCESE OF SAVANNAH.
## 1850.
### Comprises the State of Georgia and East and Middle Florida.

**BISHOP.**

Rt. Rev. JOHN BARRY, D.D., 2nd Bishop, consecrated August, 1857.

**PREDECESSOR.**

Rt. Rev. FRANCIS X. GARTLAND, 1st Bishop, consecrated Nov. 10, 1850, died in 1854. .

---

# VICARIATE APOSTOLIC OF FLORIDA.
## 1857.
### Comprising that part of Florida lying East of the Apalachicola River.

**VICAR APOSTOLIC.**

Rt. Rev. AUGUSTINE VÉROT, D.D., Bishop of Danaben, *in partibus infidelium*, consecrated April 25, 1858. Residence, St. Augustine.

---

# PROVINCE OF CINCINNATI.

The province of Cincinnati comprises the diocese of Cincinnati, Cleveland, Vincennes, Fort Wayne, Louisville, Covington, Detroit, and Saut St. Mary's, covering the States of Ohio. Indiana, Kentucky, and Michigan.

# DIOCESE OF CINCINNATI.

Established 1821.

Comprising that part of the State of Ohio lying South of 40° 41', being the counties south of the northern line of Mercer, Allen, Hardin, Marion, Knox, Coshocton, Tuscarawas, Harrison, and Jefferson counties.

#### ARCHBISHOP.

Most Rev. JOHN BAPTIST PURCELL, D.D., First Archbishop, consecrated Bishop of Cincinnati, October 13, 1833.

#### PREDECESSOR.

Rt. Rev. EDWARD FENWICK, O.S.D., D.D., consecrated in 1822; died in 1832.

---

# DIOCESE OF CLEVELAND.

1847.

Comprising that part of the State of Ohio lying North of 40° 41'.

#### BISHOP.

Rt. Rev. AMEDEUS RAPPE, D.D., 1st Bishop, consecrated October 10th, 1847.

---

# DIOCESE OF LOUISVILLE.

(1808.)

Comprising that part of KENTUCKY lying West of the Kentucky River and the Western limit of Carroll, Owen, Franklin, Woodford, Jessamine, Garrard, Rock Castle, Laurel, and Whitby Counties.

#### BISHOP.

Rt. Rev. MARTIN JOHN SPALDING, D.D., 2nd Bishop, consecrated September 10, 1848, Bishop of Lengonen, and Coadjutor to the Bishop of Louisville.

#### PREDECESSORS.

Rt. Rev. BENEDICT JOSEPH FLAGET, D.D., consecrated Bishop of Bardstown, Nov. 4, 1810; died in 1850.

Rt. Rev. JOHN B. DAVID, D.D., consecrated Bishop of Mauricastro, and Coadj. of Bardstown, Aug. 15, 1819; died in 1841.

Rt. Rev. GUY IGNATIUS CHABRAT, D.D., consecrated Bishop of Bolena and Coadj. of Bardstown, July 20, 1834; resigned in 1847.

# DIOCESE OF COVINGTON.

(1853.)

Comprising that part of KENTUCKY lying East of the Kentucky river, and of the Western limit of Carroll, Owen, Franklin, Woodford, Jessamine, Garrard, Rock Castle, Laurel, and Whitby counties.

**BISHOP.**

Rt. Rev. GEORGE ALOYSIUS CARRELL, D.D., 1st Bishop, consecrated Nov. 1, 1853.

---

# DIOCESE OF VINCENNES.

(1834.)

Embracing the Southern part of the State of INDIANA, lying south of Fountain, Montgomery, Boone, Hamilton, Madison, Delaware, Randolph, and Warren Counties.

**BISHOP.**

Rt. Rev. MAURICE DE ST. PALAIS, D.D., 4th Bishop, consecrated January 14th, 1849.

**PREDECESSORS.**

Rt. Rev. SIMON GABRIEL BRUTÉ, D.D., 1st Bishop, consecrated October 28th, 1834 ; died 1839.

Rt. Rev. CELESTINE DE LA HAILANDIERE, D.D., 2nd Bishop, consecrated August 18th, 1839 ; resigned.

Rt. Rev. JOHN BAZIN, D.D., 3rd Bishop, consecrated in 1847 ; died in 1848.

---

# DIOCESE OF FORT WAYNE.

(Jan. 8, 1857.)

Comprising Fountain, Montgomery, Boone, Hamilton, Madison, Delaware, Randolph, and Warren Counties, in the State of Indiana, and all the State lying north of them.

**BISHOP.**

Rt. Rev. JOHN H. LUERS, D.D., 1st Bishop, consecrated January 10, 1858.

---

# DIOCESE OF DETROIT.

(1832.)

Comprising the lower peninsula of the State of Michigan.

ADMINISTRATOR.

Rt. Rev. PETER PAUL LEFEVERE, D.D., consecrated Bishop of Zela, *in part.*, and coadjutor of Detroit, Nov. 21, 1841.

# DIOCESE OF SAINT MARY'S.

(1857.)

Comprising the Northern Peninsula of the State of MICHIGAN and the adjoining Islands.

BISHOP.

Rt. Rev. FREDERIC BARAGA, D.D., 1st Bishop, consecrated Bishop of Amyzonia, *in part*, Nov. 1, 1853, created Bishop of St. Mary's in 1857.

# PROVINCE OF ST. LOUIS.

The Province of St. Louis comprises the dioceses of St. Louis, Nashville, Chicago, Alton, Milwaukie, Dubuque, St. Paul, Santa Fé, the Vicariates Apostolic of Nebraska, and of Indian Territory, and embraces Missouri, Tennessee, Illinois, Wisconsin, Iowa and Minnesota, with Kansas, Nebraska, New Mexico, and Indian Territories.

# DIOCESE OF ST. LOUIS.

(July 14, 1826.)

Comprising the State of MISSOURI.

ARCHBISHOP.

Most Rev. PETER RICHARD KENRICK, D.D., 1st Archbishop, consecrated Nov. 30, 1841, Bishop of Drasa, and Coadjutor Archbishop in 1847.
Right Rev. JAMES DUGGAN, D.D., consecrated Bishop of Antigone and coadjutor of St. Louis, May 8, 1857.

BISHOP.

Right Rev. JOSEPH ROSATI, D.D., 1st Bishop of St. Louis, consecrated. March 25, 1825, Bishop of Tenagre, *in partibus*, and Coadjutor of New Orleans, transferred to St. Louis, March 27, 1827; died in 1843.

# DIOCESE OF NASHVILLE.
## (1838.)
### Embracing the State of TENNESSEE.
**BISHOP.**

Rt. Rev. RICHARD P. MILES, D.D., 1st Bishop, consecrated Sept. 16, 1838.

---

# DIOCESE OF CHICAGO.
## (1844.)
Comprising the State of ILLINOIS north of the counties of Adams, Brown, Cass, Menard, Sangamon, Macon, Moultrie, Coles, and Edgar.

**ADMINISTRATOR.**

Rt. Rev. JAMES DUGGAN, D.D., Coadjutor of St. Louis,

**PREDECESSORS.**

Rt. Rev. WILLIAM QUARTER, D.D., 1st Bishop, consecrated March 10, 1844; died in 1848.
Rt. Rev. JAMES O. VAN DE VELDE, 2nd Bishop, consecrated in 1848; Bishop of Natchez in 1853; died in 1855.
Rt. Rev. ANTHONY O'REGAN, D.D., 3d Bishop, consecrated July 25, 1854; resigned 1858.

---

# DIOCESE OF ALTON.
## (1854.)
This Diocese comprises the counties of Adams, Brown, Cass, Menard, Sangamon, Macon, Moultrie, Coles, Edgar, and that part of the State of ILLINOIS which is situated south of the above-named counties. It embraces the former Diocese of Quincy, whose See was transferred from this place to Alton by a decree of January 9th, 1857.

**BISHOP.**

Rt. Rev. HENRY DAMIAN JUNCKER, D.D., 1st Bishop, consecrated April 26th, 1857,

---

# DIOCESE OF MILWAUKEE.
## (1844.)
Comprising the State of WISCONSIN.

BISHOP.
Rt. Rev. John Martin Henni, D.D., 1st Bishop, consecrated March 19th, 1844.

# DIOCESE OF DUBUQUE.
(1837.)

Comprising the State of IOWA.

BISHOP.

Rt. Rev. Clement Smyth, D.D., Bishop of Thanasis, *in part.*, and coadj. ; consecrated May 3d, 1857.

PREDECESSOR.

Rt. Rev. Matthias Loras, D.D.,.1st Bishop, consecrated July 28th, 1837, died Feb. 19, 1858.

# DIOCESE OF ST. PAUL.
(28th June, 1850.)

Comprising the Territory of MINNESOTA.

Very Rev. A. Ravoux, Administrator.

LATE BISHOP.

Rt. Rev. Joseph Cretin, D.D., 1st Bishop, consecrated June 26th, 1851 ; died February 22d, 1857.

# VICARIATE APOSTOLIC OF THE INDIAN TERRITORY EAST OF THE ROCKY MOUNTAINS.
BISHOP.

Rt. Rev. John B. Miege, D.D., consecrated Bishop of Messenia, *in part.*, March 25th, 1851. Residence, Leavenworth City.

# VICARIATE APOSTOLIC OF NEBRASKA.
Rt. Rev. John B. Miege, D.D., Administrator.

# DIOCESE OF SANTA FE.
Embracing the Territory of NEW MEXICO.

41

BISHOP.

Rt. Rev. John Lamy, D.D., consecrated Nov. 24th, 1850, Bishop of Agathon, *in part.*, and Vicar Apostolic of New Mexico.

# PROVINCE OF NEW ORLEANS.

This Province embraces the Dioceses 'of New Orleans, Mobile, Natchez, Natchitoches, Little Rock, and Galveston, including the States of Alabama, Mississippi, Louisiana, Arkansas, and Texas.

## DIOCESE OF NEW ORLEANS.

(1793.)

Embracing the part of Louisiana between 29° and 31° N.

ARCHBISHOP.

Most Rev. Anthony Blanc, D.D., 1st Archbishop, consecrated November 22d, 1835.

PREDECESSORS.

Rt. Rev. Luis Penalver i Cardenas, 1st Bishop, transferred to Guatemala in 1802.
Rt. Rev. Francis Porro, 2d Bishop.
Rt. Rev. William V. Dubourg, 3d Bishop, consec. 24th Sept. 1815; died Archbishop of Besançon, 12th Dec. 1833.
Rt. Rev. Joseph Rosati, consec. 25th March, 1824, Bishop of Tenagre and Coadjutor of New Orleans, trans. to St. Louis, 27th March, 1827.
Rt. Rev. Leo de Neckere, 4th Bishop, consecrated in 1829; died Sept. 4th, 1833.

## DIOCESE OF MOBILE.

(1824.)

Comprising the States of ALABAMA and WEST FLORIDA.

BISHOP.

Rt. Rev. Michael Portier, D.D., 1st Bishop, consecrated Nov. 5th, 1826.

# DIOCESE OF NATCHEZ.

Comprising the State of Mississippi.

**BISHOP.**

Right Rev. WILLIAM H. ELDER, D.D., 3d Bishop, consecrated May 3, 1857.

**PREDECESSORS.**

Right Rev. JOHN J. CHANCHE, consecrated March 14, 1841; died in 1852.
Right Rev. J. O. VAN DE VELDE, D.D., transferred from Chicago in 1853;
died 1855.

# DIOCESE OF NATCHITOCHES.

(July 29th, 1853.)

Embracing all of Louisiana lying between 31° N. and 33° N.

**BISHOP.**

Rt. Rev. AUGUSTUS MARTIN, D.D., 1st Bishop, consecrated Dec. 30th, 1853.

# DIOCESE OF LITTLE ROCK.

(1843.)

Comprising the State of ARKANSAS.

**BISHOP.**

Rt. Rev. ANDREW BYRNE, D.D., 1st Bishop, consecrated March 10th, 1844.

# DIOCESE OF GALVESTON.

(1847.)

Comprising the State of TEXAS.

**BISHOP.**

Rt. Rev. JOHN MARY ODIN, D.D., 1st Bishop, consecrated March 6th, 1842,
Bishop of Claudiopolis, *in part.*, and Vic. Apost.

# PROVINCE OF SAN FRANCISCO.

Comprising the Dioceses of San Francisco and Monterey, and embracing
the State of CALIFORNIA.

# DIOCESE OF SAN FRANCISCO.
## (1853.)

Embracing CALIFORNIA N. of 37° 13' and extending to the Colorado.

### ARCHBISHOP.

Most Rev. JOSEPH SADOC ALEMANY, D.D., O.S.D , consecrated June 30, 1850, Bishop of Monterey; transferred to San Francisco, July 29, 1853.

---

# DIOCESE OF MONTEREY.
## (1840.)

Embracing Southern CALIFORNIA between 37° 13' N. and the Colorado.

### BISHOP.

Rt. Rev. THADDEUS AMAT, D.D., 3d Bishop, consecrated March 12th, 1854.

### PREDECESSORS.

Rt. Rev. FRANCIS GARCIA DIEGO, O.S.F., 1st Bishop, consecrated in 1840.
Rt. Rev. JOSEPH S. ALEMANY, D.D.,‡ 2nd Bishop, consecrated June 30th, 1850; transferred to San Francisco, July 29th, 1853.

---

# PROVINCE OF OREGON.

The Province of Oregon includes the Sees of Oregon City and Nesqualy in the United States, and Vancouver's Island in British Oregon.

---

# DIOCESE OF OREGON CITY.
## (1846.)

Comprising OREGON TERRITORY.

### ARCHBISHOP.

Most Rev. FRANCIS NORBERT BLANCHET, D.D., 1st Archbishop, consecrated Bishop of Drasa, *in part.*, July 25, 1845; transferred to Oregon City, July 24th, 1846.

---

# DIOCESE OF NESQUALY.

Comprising WASHINGTON TERRITORY.

### BISHOP.

Rt. Rev. AUGUSTINE MAGLOIRE ALEXANDER BLANCHET, D.D., consecrated Bishop of Wallawalla, Sept. 27, 1846; transferred to Nesqualy 28th July, 1850. Residence, Columbia City, Fort Vancouver.

# ARCHBISHOPS AND BISHOPS IN THE BRITISH PROVINCES.

## PROVINCE OF QUEBEC.

Most Rev. Peter F. Turgeon, D.D., Archbishop of Quebec.
Rt. Rev. C. F. Baillargeon, D.D., Bishop of Tloa, Coad. and Admr.
Rt. Rev. Thomas Cooke, D.D., Bishop of Three Rivers.
Rt. Rev. John Charles Prince, D.D., Bishop of St. Hyacinth.
Rt. Rev. Ignatius Bourget, D.D., Bishop of Montreal.
Rt. Rev. J. Larocque, D.D., Bishop of Cydonia, Coadjutor.
Rt. Rev. Joseph E. B. Guigues, D.D, Bishop of Bytown.
Rt. Rev. Edward Horan, D.D., Bishop of Kingston.
Rt. Rev. Armand F. M. de Charbonnel, D.D., Bishop of Toronto.
Rt. Rev. John Farrell, D.D., Bishop of Hamilton.
Rt. Rev. P. A. Pinsoneault, D.D., Bishop of London.
Rt. Rev. A. Taché, D.D., Bishop of St. Boniface.

## PROVINCE OF OREGON.

Rt. Rev. Modest Demers, D.D., Bishop of Vancouver's Island.

## PROVINCE OF HALIFAX.

Most Rev. ——— Archbishop of Halifax. (See vacant.)
Rt. Rev. T. L. Connolly, D.D., Bishop of St. John, N. B.
Rt. Rev. Colin Francis McKinnon, D.D., Bishop of Arichat.
Rt. Rev. John Dalton, D.D., Bishop of Harbor Grace.
Rt. Rev. B. D. McDonald, D D., Bishop of Charlottetown, (P. E.)
Rt. Rev. J. F. Mullock, O.S.F., Bishop of Newfoundland.

## PROVINCE OF PORT OF SPAIN.

Most Rev. Mgr. Spaccapietra, D.D., Archbishop of Port of Spain.
Rt. Rev. J. Du Peyron, D.D., V. A. of Jamaica, Bahama, Honduras, and Yucatan.
Rt. Rev. ———, D.D., Bishop of Roseau. (See vacant.)
Rt. Rev. John T. Hynes, D.D., Bishop of Leros, V. A. of Guiana.
Rt. Rev. James Etheridge, D.D., Bishop of Torone and V. A. of Demarara.

# CATHOLIC THEOLOGICAL SEMINARIES AND NOVITIATES OF REGULARS IN THE UNITED STATES.

St. Joseph's Theological Seminary.............Fordham, N. Y.
Ecclesiastical Seminary....................Buffalo,    "
Franciscan Convent.........................Alleghany, "
Theol. Seminary of St. Charles Borromeo.......Philadelphia, Pa.
Augustinian Monastery of St. Thomas..........Villa Nova,   "
Benedictine Monastery of St. Vincent..........near Latrobe, "
Passionist Convent of Blessed Paul............Birmingham, "
St. Mary's Theological Seminary...............Baltimore, Maryland.
Novitiate of the Society of Jesus.............Frederick,   "
Mt. St. Mary's Theological Seminary...........near Emmitsburg, Md.
House of Studies of Redemptorists ............Cumberland,   "
Ecclesiastical Seminary.....................Wheeling, Va.
Ecclesiastical Seminary.....................Charleston, S. C.
Mount St. Mary's Eccl. Seminary..............near Cincinnati, Ohio
Dominican Convent of St. Joseph's............near Somerset, O.
Dominican Convent of St. Rose...............near Springfield, Ky.
Diocesan Seminary of St. Thomas..............near Bardstown, "
St. Mary's Ecclesiastical Seminary............Cleveland, Ohio.
Congregation Pretiosissimi Sanguinis..........Thompson,   "
St Charles' Ecclesiastical Seminary...........near Vincennes, Indiana.
University of Notre-Dam-du-Lac...............Notre-Dame.
Ecclesiastical Seminary of St. Vincent of Paul ...New Orleans, La.
Theological Seminary of St. Louis.............Carondolet, Mo.
Novitiate of Society of Jesus.................near Florisant, Mo.
Ecclesiastical Seminary.....................Springhill, Ala.
Eccles. Seminary of St. Francis of Sales ........Milwaukee, Wis.
Seminary ...............................Dubuque, Iowa.
St. Thomas Aquinas' Seminary................San Francisco, Cal.
Dominican Convent .......................Benicia, California.
Seminary of Na. Sa. de Guadalupe ............Santa Ines,  "
College for the Propagation of the Faith.......Santa Barbara, Cal.
St. Mary's Seminary........................Galveston.

# PREPARATORY SEMINARIES.

Preparatory Seminary of our Lady of the Angels..Niagara, N. Y.
St. Charles' College.......................near Ellicott's Mills, Md.
St. Mary's Preparatory Seminary..............Barrens, Perry co., Mo.
Novitiate of Redemptorists....................Annapolis, Md.
Preparatory Seminary of St. Thomas...........near Bardstown, Ky.
Seminary.....................................Milwaukee, Wisconsin.
Preparatory Seminary of San Francisco .... ....Santa Fe, N. M.

# CATHOLIC COLLEGES IN THE UNITED STATES.

Georgetown College.........................Georgetown, D. C.
Mt. St. Mary's College......................near Emmitsburg, Md.
St. John's College..........................Fordham, N. Y.
College of St. Francis Xavier................New York city.
College of the Holy Cross....................Worcester, Mass.
Seton Hall College..........................Madison, N. J.
St. Mary's College..........................Wilmington, Del.
Augustinian College.........................Villa Nova, Pa.
St. Joseph's College.........................Philadelphia, Pa.
St. John's College..........................Frederick, Md.
Loyola College..............................Baltimore, Md.
St. Xavier College..........................Cincinnati, Ohio.
Mount St. Mary's College....................near Cincinnati, O.
St. Joseph's College.........................Somerset, O.
St. Joseph's College.........................Bardstown, Ky.
St. Mary's College..........................near Lebanon, Ky.
St. Stanislaus College.......................Scott Co., Ky.
University of Notre-Dame-du-Lac.............Notre Dame, Ind.
St. Charles' College.........................Grand Coteau, La.
College of SS. Peter and Paul...............Baton Rouge, La.
College of the Immaculate Conception........New Orleans, La.
University of St. Louis......................St. Louis, Mo.
St. Vincent's College........................Cape Girardeau, Mo.
University of St. Mary of the Lake...........Chicago, Ill.
Springhill College..........................Springhill, Ala.
St. Joseph's College.........................Susquehanna, Pa.
Sinsinawa Mound College....................Sinsinawa, Wis.
College of St. Andrew.......................near Fort Smith, Ark
Santa Clara College.........................Santa Clara Cal.
St. Mary's College .........................Columbia, S. C.

# GOVERNMENT OF THE UNITED STATES.

JAMES BUCHANAN, of Pennsylvania......President................Salary, $25,000
JOHN C. BRECKENRIDGE, of Tennessee,.Vice-President...........Salary, 8,000

## THE CABINET.

LEWIS CASS, of Michigan,................Secretary of State,........Salary, $8,000
HOWELL COBB, of Georgia..............Sec'y of the Treasury,......Salary, 8,000
JOHN B. FLOYD, of Virginia,......... ...Secretary of War,.........Salary, 8,000
ISAAC TOUCEY, of Connecticut,.........Secretary of the Navy,......Salary, 8,000
JACOB THOMPSON, of Mississippi, ......Sec'y of the Interior.......Salary, 8,000
AARON V. BROWN, of Tennessee,.........Postmaster General,........Salary, 8,000
JAMES BLACK, of Pennsylvania,.........Attorney General,.........Salary, 8,000

## THE SUPREME COURT.

ROGER B. TANEY, of Maryland, Chief Justice.  Salary, $6,500.

| John M'Lean, of Ohio, | Peter V. Daniel, of Virginia, | John A. Campbell, of Ala., |
| James M. Wayne, of Georgia, | Samuel Nelson, of N. York, | Nathan Clifford, of Me., |
| John Katron, of Tennessee, | Robert C. Grier, of Penn., | Assoc'te Justices, Sal'y $6,000. |

The Supreme Court is held at Washington on the first Monday in December in each year.
The United States are divided into ten Judicial Circuits, in each of which a Circuit Court is held semi-annually, by a Justice of the Supreme Court and the District Judge of the State or District in which the court sits.

## THE SENATE

Is composed of two members elected by the Legislature of each State for the term of six years.  Their terms are so arranged, that one third expire every two years.  The Vice-President presides in the Senate, and in case of an equal division has a casting vote.

| MAINE. | PENNSYLVANIA. | ALABAMA. | MISSOURI. |
|---|---|---|---|
| W. P. Fessenden 1859 | William Bigler..1861 | Benj. Fitzpatrick1861 | James S. Green..1861 |
| Hannibal Hamlin 1863 | Simon Cameron.1863 | Clement C. Clay 1863 | Trusten Polk....1863 |
| **NEW-HAMPSHIRE.** | **DELAWARE.** | **MISSISSIPPI.** | **ARKANSAS.** |
| John P. Hale....1859 | Martin W. Bates 1859 | A. G. Brown....1859 | W. K. Sebastian.1859 |
| Daniel Clark....1861 | James A. Bayard 1861 | Jefferson Davis..1863 | R. W. Johnson..1861 |
| **VERMONT.** | **MARYLAND.** | **LOUISIANA.** | **MICHIGAN.** |
| Jacob Collamer..1861 | James A. Pearce 1861 | J. P. Benjamin..1859 | Chas. E. Stuart..1859 |
| Solomon Foote .1863 | Anth. Kennedy ..1863 | John Slidell.....1861 | Zacha. Chandler.1863 |
| **MASSACHUSETTS.** | **VIRGINIA.** | **TENNESSEE.** | **TEXAS.** |
| Henry Wilson...1859 | R. M. T. Hunter.1859 | John Bell......1859 | Sam. Houston...1859 |
| Charles Sumner.1863 | James M. Mason 1863 | A. Johnson......1861 | J. P. Henderson.1861 |
| **RHODE ISLAND.** | **NORTH CAROLINA.** | **KENTUCKY.** | **IOWA.** |
| Philip Allen.....1859 | David S. Reid...1859 | J. B. Thompson..1859 | George W. Jones 1859 |
| Jas. F. Simmons.1863 | T. L. Clingman..1861 | J. J. Crittenden..1861 | James Harlan...1861 |
| **CONNECTICUT.** | **SOUTH CAROLINA.** | **OHIO.** | **WISCONSIN.** |
| L. S. Foster.....1861 | 1859 | George E. Pugh.1861 | Charles Durkee..1861 |
| James Dixon....1863 | J. H. Hammond.1861 | Benj. F. Wade...1863 | Jas. R. Doolittle 1863 |
| **NEW YORK.** | **GEORGIA.** | **INDIANA.** | **CALIFORNIA.** |
| Wm. H. Seward.1861 | Alfred Iverson..1861 | ———........1861 | Wm. M. Gwin...1861 |
| Preston King....1863 | Robert Toombs..1863 | ———......1863 | D. C. Broderick..1863 |
| **NEW JERSEY.** | **FLORIDA.** | **ILLINOIS.** | NOTE.—The figures de- |
| William Wright.1859 | Steph. R.Mallory 1859 | Step. A. Douglas 1859 | note the period when each |
| J. R. Thomson...1863 | David L. Yulce..1861 | Lyman Trumbull 1861 | senator's term expires. |

# STATE OFFICE AND TERRITORIAL GOVERNMENTS.

| States. | Capitals. | Governors. | Term Exp. | Salary. | Legislat're meets. |
|---|---|---|---|---|---|
| Alabama..... | Montgomery ......... | Andrew B. Moore. | Dec. 1859 | $2,500 | 2 M. Nov. |
| Arkansas..... | Little Rock........... | Elias N. Conway.. | Nov.1860 | 1,800 | 1 M. Nov. |
| California .... | Sacramento ......... | John B. Weller.. | Dec. 1859 | 10,000 | 1 M. Jan. |
| Connecticut .. | Hartford and N. Haven | Alex. H. Holley .. | May 1858 | 1,000 | 1 W. May. |
| Delaware .... | Dover............... | Peter F. Causey .. | Jan. 1859 | 1,333 | 1 Tu. June. |
| Florida ...... | Tallahassee.......... | Marshall S. Perry. | Nov. 1861 | 1,500 | 1 M. Nov. |
| Georgia ..... | Milledgeville. ....... | Joseph E. Brown . | Nov. 1859 | 3,000 | 1 M. Nov. |
| Illinois ...... | Springfield........... | William H. Bissell | Jan. 1861 | 1,500 | 2 M. Jan. |
| Indiana ...... | Indianapolis.......... | Ashbel P. Willard. | Jan. 1861 | 1,800 | January. |
| Iowa......... | Des Moines ......... | Ralph P. Lowe.... | Jan. 1860 | 1,000 | 2 M. Jan. |
| Kentucky .... | Frankfort........... | Chas S. Morehead. | Aug. 1859 | 2,500 | 1 M. Dec. |
| Louisiana .... | Baton Rouge ......... | R. C. Wickliffe.... | Jan. 1860 | ..... | 3 M. Jan. |
| Maine........ | Augusta............. | Lot M. Morrill.... | Jan. 1859 | 1,500 | 1 W. Jan. |
| Maryland..... | Annapolis ............ | Thomas H. Hicks. | Jan. 1862 | 3,600 | 1 W. Jan. |
| Massachusetts. | Boston ............. | Nath. P. Banks.. | Jan. 1859 | 2,500 | 1 W. Jan. |
| Michigan ..... | Lansing ............. | K. S. Bingham.... | Jan. 1859 | 1,500 | 1 W. Jan. |
| Minnesota.... | St. Paul ............ | Henry H. Sibley... | ........ | ..... | |
| Mississippi... | Jackson . ..\.......... | William M'Willie. | Jan. 1860 | 3,000 | 1 M. Jan. |
| Missouri ..... | Jefferson City......... | Robert M. Stewart | Dec. 1860 | 2,000 | Last M. Dec. |
| N. Hampshire. | Concord............ | William Haile.... | June 1858 | 1,000 | 1 W. June. |
| New Jersey .. | Trenton............. | William A. Newell | Jan. 1860 | 1,800 | 2 Tu. June. |
| New York ... | Albany............. | John A. King..... | Jan. 1859 | 4,000 | 1 Tu. June. |
| N. Carolina... | Raleigh ........... | Thomas Bragg.... | Jan. 1859 | 2,000 | 3 M. Nov. |
| Ohio ......... | Columbus ........... | Salmon P. Chase.. | Jan. 1860 | 1,800 | 1 M. Jan. |
| Pennsylvania. | Harrisburgh......... | William F. Packer | Jan. 1861 | 3,500 | 1 Tu. Jan. |
| Rhode Island. | Newport & Providence | Elisha Dyer....... | May 1858 | 400 | May & Oct. |
| S. Carolina ... | Columbia ........... | R. F. W. Allston.. | Dec 1858 | 3,500 | 4 M. Nov. |
| Tennessee.... | Nashville ........... | Isham G. Harris.. | Oct. 1859 | 2,000 | 1 M. Oct. |
| Texas........ | Austin ............. | Hardin R.Runnells | Dec. 1861 | 3,000 | In Decemb. |
| Vermont ..... | Montpelier ......... . | Ryland Fletcher.. | Oct. 1858 | 750 | 2 Th. Oct. |
| Virginia...... | Richmond........... | Henry A. Wise ... | Jan. 1860 | 5,000 | 2 M. Jan. |
| Wisconsin .... | Madison ........... | Alex. W. Randall. | Dec. 1859 | 1,250 | 1 M. Jan. |

## GOVERNORS OF TERRITORIES.

| Territories. | Capitals. | Governors. |
|---|---|---|
| Kansas...,............. | Lecompton................. | James W. Denver. |
| Nebraska........·····..... | ...................... | William A. Richardson. |
| New Mexico.............. | Santa Fé................. | Abraham Rencher. |
| Oregon................... | Oregon City.............. | George L. Curry. |
| Utah.................,..... | Salt Lake... ............. | Alfred Cumming. |
| Washington..............,..... | ..................,...... | Fayette M'Mullen. |

# CATHOLIC PERIODICALS,

PUBLISHED IN THE UNITED STATES.

## WEEKLY.

*The New York Freeman's Journal and Catholic Register*, published every Saturday in the city of New York. Terms, $3 in advance, by carrier; by mail, $2 50 in advance, after 6 months, $3. J. A. McMaster, Editor.

*The New York Tablet*, published every Saturday. Terms, $3 by carrier; $2 50 by mail. D. & J. Sadlier, Publishers.

*The United States Catholic Miscellany*, published every Saturday in Charleston, S. C., at $3 per annum. With the approbation of the Right Rev. the Bishop of Charleston.

*Catholic Telegraph and Advocate*, published every Saturday in Cincinnati, by John P. Walsh. Terms, $2 in advance; delivered to subscribers, $2 50. Edited by V. Rev. Edward Purcell and Rev. S. Rosecrans, D.D., with the approbation of the Most Rev. Archbishop of Cincinnati.

*The Catholic Herald and Visitor*, published every Thursday in Philadelphia, $2 50 per annum, in advance; otherwise, $3. Edited by Joseph R. Chandler, with the approbation of the Bishop of Philadelphia.

*Le Propagateur Catholique* (French paper), published every Saturday in New Orleans, La., by H. Meridier. Terms, $4 50 per annum, by carrier; by mail, $4; otherwise, 50 cents are added. With the approbation of the Most Rev. the Archbishop of New Orleans.

*The Pittsburg Catholic*, published every Saturday, by Jacob Porter, Pittsburg, Pa., at $1 per annum, in advance; otherwise, $1 50. With the approbation of the Rt. Rev. the Bishop of Pittsburg.

*The Catholic Mirror*, published every Saturday, by P. J. Hédian, Baltimore, with the approbation of the Most Rev. Archbishop. Terms, $2 per annum for distant subscribers; for those in the city, $2 50.

*The Pilot*, published every Saturday at Boston and New York. Terms, $2 50 per annum, in advance. Pat. Donahoe, publisher and proprietor.

*Der Herold Des Glaubers*, published every Saturday at St. Louis, Mo.

*Der Warheit's Freund* (German paper), published every Thursday, in Cincinnati, Ohio, at $2 50 per annum. With the approbation of the Most Rev. the Archbishop of Cincinnati.

*Der Religion's Freund* (German), published every Thursday morning at Baltimore, Md.

*Katholische Kirchen Zeitung* (German), published in New York every

Friday, at $2 per annum. With the approbation of the Most Rev. Archbishop. Edited by Maximilian Œrtel, Esq.

*The Buffalo Sentinel*, published every Saturday, at Buffalo, N. Y., by Michael Hagan. Terms, $2 per annum, in advance. With the approbation of the Rt. Rev. Bishop.

*The Catholic Standard*, published every Sunday, at New Orleans, by Jas. A. Kennedy, Editor, 184 Camp-st. Terms, $3 in advance. With the approbation of the Most Rev. Archbishop.

*The Western Star*, published at Dubuque, Iowa.

*The Guardian*, published at Louisville, Ky., by Webb, Gill, and Levering.

*The Monitor*, published in San Francisco, Cal., by Marks, Thompson & Co., at $5 per annum.

## MONTHLY.

*The Metropolitan*, a monthly Magazine, devoted to Religion, Education, Literature, and General Information. Published by John Murphy & Co., 182 Market street, Baltimore. Edited by M. J. Kerney, Esq. Terms, $2 in advance.

*The Catholic Youth's Magazine*, published by John Murphy & Co., Baltimore. With the approbation of the Most Rev. Archbishops of Baltimore and Cincinnati. Terms, 50 cents per annum.

*The Catholic Institute Magazine*, Newburgh, N.Y. 50 cents per annum.

*Theodora, or Immortal Crowns for Soul and Heart*, a German Catholic Monthly Magazine, published in Springfield, Illinois.

## QUARTERLY.

*Brownson's Quarterly Review*, devoted to religion, philosophy, and general literature. Published in New York, by Edward Dunigan & Brother, for the proprietor, on the 1st of January, April, July, and October. Terms, $3 per annum, in advance.

## ANNUAL.

*Ordo Divini Officii Recitandi, Missæque Celebrandæ*, juxta rubricas breviarii ac missalis Romani. Published by Lucas Brothers, Baltimore.

*Ordo Divini Officii Recitandi*, published by John P. Walsh, Cincinnati, Ohio.

*The American Catholic Almanac and Clergy List*, published by Edward Dunigan and Brother, New York,

*The Six Cent Catholic Almanac and Lady's Directory*, published by Edward Dunigan and Brother, New York,

## OBITUARY, 1858.

*February* 19.—*Rt. Rev. Matthias Loras, D.D.*, Bishop of Dubuque, in his 67th year.

*January* 23.—*Rev. Michael Calvo*, of the congregation of the Missions at the Maison de Santé, New Orleans, aged 45, in the 20th year of his priesthood.

*February* 5.—*Rev. Patrick M'Kenna*, late pastor of St. James' Church, New York, at New York in his 40th year.

*February* —.—*Rev. Peter F. Ladivière*, of the Society of Jesus, at Spring Hill College, near Mobile.

*March* 5.—*Rev. Joseph Lenon*, at Mount Hope, near Baltimore.

*March* 9.—*Rev. John Henry Forstman*, Peoria, Illinois, in his 65th year.

*April* 2.—*Rev. Matthias Wurtz*, of the diocese of Cincinnati, at Metz,France.

*April* —.—*Rev. John Ryan*, of the diocese of Buffalo, aged 30.

*April* 11.—*Rev. Nicholas Prunier*, on board of the Fulton, aged 37.

*April* 13.—*Rev. Michael Doherty*, at Tuscaloosa, Ala., aged 26.

*April* 23.—*Rev. Francis Bucaut*, of the cong. of the most Holy Redeemer.

*April* 24.—*Rev. John Bilstein*, at Minster, O., in his 28th year.

*June* —.—*Rev. James Gallagher*, pastor of Elgin, Ill., drowned.

*June* 10.—*Rev William O'Brien*, at Oak Creek, Wis., in his 60th year

*June* 13.—*Rev. Anthony Urbanek*, of Milwaukee, aged 37.

*June* 14.—*Rev. J. L. Delcross*, of Bouligny, La., killed by the bursting of the boiler of the steamer Pennsylvania, near Memphis.

*June* 25.—*Rev. Father Maria Placidus*, Trappist, monk of Gethsemane, aged 54.

*July* 12.—*Rev. J. B. Kramer*, at Erie, by poison inadvertently taken.

*July* 18.—*Rev. William Barrett*, pastor of St. Thomas' Church, Cincinnati, at Cincinnati, aged 29.

*Aug.* 5.—*Rev. John Otho Brederick*, at Delphos, O., in 70th year of his age and 36th of his priesthood.

*Aug.* 23.—*Rev. Thomas M'Evoy*, of diocese of Buffalo, at N.Y., aged —

*Aug.* 20.—*Rev. Dominic Moro*, at New Orleans, of yellow fever.

*February* —.—Sis. *Clotilda O'Reilly*, sis. of St. Joseph, at M'Sherrystown.

*Feb.* 26.—Sis. *Mary Liguori* (Ellen C. Duffy), Ursuline, at Cleveland, O.

*March* 14.—Sister *Mary Catharine* (Catharine M'Grath), sister of Charity at Mount Hope.

*March* 18 —Sister *Mary Teresa* (Mary Anne Murray), sister of Mercy, at Hartford.

*March* 20.—Mother *Catharine Spalding*, superioress of the sisters of Charity, in Kentucky, at Louisville, in her 65th year.

*March* 30.—Brother *Stephen Castillo* of the order of St. Francis, at Loretto, Penn.

*July* 26.—Sister *William Anna* (Fagan), sister of Charity, at St. John's Hospital, Cincinnati, in her 27th year.

*August* 2.———— *Meyer*, Scholastic of the society of Jesus, at St. Joseph's College, Bardstown, Ky.

*Aug.* 19.—Sis. *Mary Elizabeth* (Mahoney) Ursuline, at St. Martin's, O., in her 35th year.

*Aug.* 25.—Sister *Mary Magdalen* (Elizabeth Bartley), Sister of our Lady of Mercy, at Charleston, in the 73d year of her age.

# CATHOLIC CHURCHES IN THE CITY OF NEW YORK.

ARCHBISHOP.

Most Rev. JOHN HUGHES, D.D., Archbishop of New York.
Very Rev. William Starrs, Vic-Gen.
Very Rev. Michael McCurran, Archdeacon.

COUNCILLORS.

Rev. THOS. MARTIN, O.S.D.; Rev. J. W. CUMMINGS, D.D.; Rev. WM. QUINN; Rev. THOS. S. PRESTON, Ch.

Office, 81 Marion street—open from 10 A.M. to 12 M., where all applications for dispensations must be sent.

Cathedral of St. Patrick—Mott street, between Prince and Houston. Archiepiscopal residence, 263 Mulberry street. *Very Rev. William Starrs*, Vic. Gen., Rector. *Rev. Thos. S Preston*, Chan. *Rev. Francis McNeirny*, Secretary. *Rev. John Barry. Rev. John McEvoy. Rev. P. Hennessy*—Who attends Calvary Cemetery. High Mass at 10½ A.M.; Vespers at 3½ P.M.

St. Peter's—Barclay street—Residence, 15 Barclay. *Rev. William Quinn' Rev. Jas. L. Conron, Rev. John Shanahan.* High Mass at 10½ A.M.; Vespers at 3½ P.M.

St. Mary's—Corner Grand and Ridge streets—Residence, 11 Ridge street. *Very Rev. Michael McCarron, Rev. Peter McCarron, Rev. James Boyce.* High Mass at 10½ A.M.; Vespers at 3½ P.M.

St. Joseph's—6th Avenue, corner of Barrow street—Residence, 67 6th avenue. *Rev. Thomas Farrell, Rev. Jerome Nobriga, Rev. Hugh Brady.* High Mass at 10½ A.M.; Vespers at 3½ P.M.

**St. James—James street—Residence, 23 Oliver street. *Rev. Thomas Martin*, O S.D., *Rev. James Brennan, Rev. Claudius Pernot.* High Mass at 10½ A.M.; Vespers at 3½ P.M.**

**Transfiguration—Mott street, near Chatham—Residence, 30 Mott street. *Rev. William McClellan, Rev. Thomas Treanor.* High Mass at 10½ A.M.; Vespers at 3½ P.M.**

**St. Nicholas, (German)—2d street, near avenue A—Residence, 135 Second street. *Rev. Ambrose Buchmeyer, Rev. Felician Krebez.* High Mass at 10½ A.M.; Vespers at 3 P.M.**

**St. Andrew's—Duane street, corner City Hall Place—Residence, 13 City Hall Place. *Rev. Michael Curran, Rev. Louis Terykowich.* High Mass at 10½ A.M.; Vespers at 3½ P.M.**

Church of the Nativity—Second avenue—Residence, 44 2d avenue. *Rev. George McCloskey, Rev. William Everett.* High Mass at 10 A.M. ; Vespers at 3 P.M.

St. Vincent de Paul, (French)—West 23d st. near 6th avenue—Residence, 90 24th street. *Rev. Annet Lafont,* S.P.M., *Rev. Almire Fourmont,* P S.M., *Rev. Louis Gamboville,* P.S.M. High Mass at 10¼ A.M.; Vespers at 3½ P M.

Church of the Most Holy Redeemer, (German)—Third street—Res. 153 3d street. *Rev. J. M. Helmpracht,* C.SS.R., and the Fathers of his order; High Mass at 10 A.M; Vespers at 3 P.M.

St. John the Baptist, (German)—Thirtieth street, between 7th and 8th avenues—Residence, 127 W. 30th street. *Rev. Augustine Dantner.* High Mass at 10¼ A.M. ; Vespers at 3½ P.M.

St. Columba's—25th street, near 8th avenue—Residence, 215 W. 25th street. *Rev. Michael McAleer, Rev. Titus Joslin.* High Mass at 10¼ A.M.; Vespers at 3½ P.M.

St. Francis, (German)—31st street, between 6th and 7th avenues—Residence, 89 W. 31st street. *Rev. Alexander Martin,* O.S.F., *Rev. Fred. Chas. Rudolph.* High Mass at 10¼ A.M. ; Vespers at 3½ P.M.

St. Alphonsus, (German)—Thompson street—Served from the Redemptorists' Convent, by *Rev. Fred. Lutte,* C.SS.R. High Mass at 10¼ A.M. ; Vespers at 3½ P.M.

St. John Evangelist—50th street. *Rev. James McMahon, Rev. Alfred J. Dayman.*

St. Paul's, Harlem—117th street. *Rev. George Brophy.*

St. Bridget's—Avenue B, corner 8th street—Residence, 111 Avenue B. *Rev. Thomas Mooney, Rev. Charles Slevin.* High Mass at 10¼ A.M.; Vespers at 3½ P.M.

St. Stephen's—28th street, between Lexington and 3d avenues. Residence, 80 E. 29th street. *Rev. J. W. Cummings,* D.D., *Rev. Wm. Clowry, Rev. J. Z. Doyle.* High Mass at 10 A.M.; Vespers at 3½ P.M.

St. Francis Xavier's—16th street, between 5th and 6th avenues. Residence, 39 W. 15th street. *Rev. M. Driscol,* S J., *Rev. W. Moylan,* S J., *Rev. H. de Luynes,* S.J. High Mass at 10¼ A.M.; Vespers at 3½ P. M. Mass and instruction in chapel for boys, 8 A.M.

St. Anthony of Padua, (Italian)—Canal street. *Rev. A. Sanguinetti.* High Mass at 10¼ A.M.; Vespers at 3½ P.M.

St. Ann's—8th street, between Broadway and 4th Avenue. *Rev. John M. Forbes,* D.D., *Rev. Peter Murphy, Rev. M. Nicot.* High Mass at 10¼ A.M. ; Vespers at 3½ P.M.

Church of the Immaculate Conception, 14th street. Residence, 243 14th street. *Rev. John Ryan, Rev. E. Maguire.* High Mass at 10¼ A.M.; Vespers at 3½ P.M.

St. Lawrence's—84th street. *Rev. Walter J. Quarter.* High Mass at 10¼ A.M.; Vespers at 3¼ P.M.

Church of the Holy Cross—42d street, between 8th and 9th avenues. Residence, 211 W. 42d street. *Rev. Patrick McCarthy, Rev. Patrick Eagan.* High Mass at 10¼ A M.; Vespers at 3¼ P.M.

Church of the Annunciation B.V.M., Manhattanville. *Rev. F. H. Farelly.*

St. Michael's—W. 31st street, near Ninth avenue. Residence, 270 W. 31st street. *Rev. Arthur J. Donnelly, Rev. D. Teixchera.* High Mass at 10¼ A.M.; Vespers at 3¼ P.M.

New Church. Not Blessed—9th avenue, between 59th and 60th streets. *Rev. Isaac T. Hecker, Rev. Francis A. Baker, Rev. George Deshon, Rev. A. H. Hewit,* of the Congregation of Missionaries of St. Paul.

Church of the Assumption, (German)—Corner of 9th avenue and 50th street. *Rev. M——.*

Mount St. Vincent, Mother House of the Sisters of Charity—107th street, between 5th and 6th avenues. *Rev. M. Breen.*

Convent of the Sacred Heart—Manhattanville. *Rev. Jeremiah Donovan,* D.D.

St. Catharine's Convent of the Sisters of Mercy—Corner of Houston and Mulberry streets. *Rev. Thomas S. Preston.*

House of the Good Shepherd—191 East 14th street. *Rev. M. Nicot.*

Ward's Island. *Rev. Ambrose Manahan,* D.D.

Blackwell's Island. *Rev. M. Joyce.*

City Prison, visited from St. Francis Xavier's College.

## CATALOGUE OF NEW AND CHEAP

# Standard Catholic Publications.

---

### THE OLD ESTABLISHED CATHOLIC HOUSE OF

## EDWARD DUNIGAN & BROTHER,

### (JAMES B. KIRKER,)

### No. 371 Broadway, New York,

Invite the attention of the Catholic Hierarchy and Clergy, Colleges, Convents, Religious Institutions, Catholic Institutes, Parish and Free Schools, and the public generally, to the annexed Catalogue. The prices are the retail prices, from which a large discount is made to the trade and Catholic Institutions.
*Any work in the within Catalogue sent by Mail, free of postage, on receipt of the price annexed. Copies of School Books for examination sent free of postage.*

---

### COPY OF A LETTER

#### Accompanying a Gold Medal sent by the Holy Father,

### TO EDWARD DUNIGAN & BROTHER.

Most worthy and respected Gentlemen:

Some books, which, as it appeared by your most courteous letter, you wished to offer to our most holy Lord Pope Pius IX., have been lately handed to him. This act on your part could not but please his Holiness, and the zeal you constantly show by the publication of works in defence and protection of the cause of the Catholic Religion, gives him great joy.

The Sovereign Pontiff, therefore, with great pleasure encourages you in your course by this letter, and returns you his thanks for the gift which you offer.

I am, moreover, ordered to transmit a Gold Medal, which the same benign Pontiff sends, impressed with his august effigy, and with it, as a pledge of his paternal and especial affection towards you, his Apostolic blessing, which, as an auspice of all heavenly good, he lovingly grants you with the most sincere affection of his heart.

I have only to profess my respects to you, Gentlemen, on whom I earnestly implore all that is saving and propitious from our Lord.

Gentlemen,

Your most humble and obedient Servant,

DOMINIC FIORAMONTI,

Rome, July 6th, 1853.  Latin Secretary to his Holiness.

To E. DUNIGAN & BROTHER, New York.

# ST. JOHN'S MANUAL:

### A GUIDE TO THE

### 𝔓ublic 𝔚o.ship and 𝔖erbices

#### OF

# THE CATHOLIC CHURCH

#### AND A

## COLLECTION OF DEVOTIONS

#### FOR THE PRIVATE USE OF THE FAITHFUL.

---

ST. JOHN'S MANUAL is, it is hoped, the most complete and accurate prayer book ever offered to the Catholic community in the United States. Many of the present books of devotion being reprints of European works, are far from conforming to the Roman office books as authorized for use in this country, and are devoid of such explanations as enable the uninstructed to follow our service. The St. John's Manual conforms strictly to the rules of the Holy See in this regard.

In a word, the compilers have conscientiously endeavored to draw from the holy service books of the Church, as published by the authority of the Councils of Baltimore, from the works of her canonized Saints, and approved ascetics and theologians, such prayers and instructions as may meet the wants of the faithful, and render this Manual the best and most complete Catholic Prayer Book for devotional and family use yet published.

In a material point of view, St. John's Manual has been got up in the best style; printed on paper of surpassing fineness, from new type expressly selected, and is adorned with Vignettes designed for and appropriate to the work. The steel engravings, by Muller of Dusseldorf, are of an entirely new character, illustrating the Sacraments and Rites of the Church. The work itself, of which the contents are annexed, is intended not only to furnish a manual of the most approved prayers and devotions for health and sickness, but also to give the offices and ceremonies of the Church, with such explanations as will enable all to follow them.

## CONTENTS OF ST. JOHN'S MANUAL.

Calendar.
Moveable Feasts, &c.
Summary of Christian Doctrine; of Prayer.
Morning Exercise and Prayers.
Meditation, on Mental Prayer.
On Sanctifying Study.
Manner of Spending the Day.
Evening Exercise and Prayers.
Family Prayers for Morning and Evening.
Morning and Evening Prayers for every day in the week.
Instruction on the Holy Sacrifice of the Mass; Prayers before Mass.
The Ordinary of the MASS, with full explanations.
Prayers at Mass.
Devotions for Mass, by way of Meditation on the Passion.
Mass in Union with the Sacred Heart of Jesus.
Prayers at Mass for the Dead.
Method of Hearing Mass spiritually, for those who cannot attend actually.
Collects, Epistles, and Gospels for all the Sundays and Holidays, including the Ceremonies of Holy Week, with explanations of the Festivals and Seasons.
VESPERS, with full explanation.

Benediction of the Blessed Sacrament, with Instructions.
The Office of Tenebræ.
An ample Instruction on the Sacrament of PENANCE; Preparation and Prayers before Confession; Examination of Conscience; Prayers after Confession; Devotions after Confession.
Instructions and Devotions for HOLY COMMUNION—Prayers before and after Communion —Prayers for Mass before Communion—Mass of Thanksgiving after Communion; Instruction and Prayers for first Communion.
Instruction and Prayers for Confirmation; Order of Confirmation.
Devotions to the Holy Trinity; Devotions to the Holy Ghost.   .
Devotions to the Sacred Humanity of our Lord—the Holy Name—the Infant Jesus—the Passion—the Holy Eucharist—the Sacred Heart.
Devotions to the Blessed Virgin; Little Office—Office of the Immaculate Conception— Rosary—St. Liguori's Prayers for every day in the week.
Devotions to the Holy Angels; Devotions to the Saints, general and particular.
Devotions for particular seasons and circumstances—for the Pope—the Church—the Authorities—for the Conversion of those in Error—the Itinerary—Prayers for time of Pestilence—Universal Prayer, &c., &c.
Prayers for various states of life—for Children—the Married, the Single, &c.—Instructions on Matrimony and the Marriage Service—Churching of Women—Instruction and Order of Baptism, &c., &c.—Devotions for a happy death.
Morning and Evening Prayers—Instructions—Ejaculations—Order of the Visitation of the Sick—Prayers before and after Confession and Communion—Order of administering the Holy Viaticum—Instruction on Extreme Unction—Order of administering it—Last Blessing and Plenary Indulgence—Order of Commending the departing Soul.
The Office of the Dead—the Burial Service for Adults and Infants—Prayers for the Faithful Departed.
Manner of receiving Profession from a Convert.
Litanies—of the Saints—of Faith, Hope, Charity, Penance, and Thanksgiving, by Pope Pius VI.—of the Most Holy Trinity—Infant Jesus—Life of Christ—Passion—Cross —Blessed Sacrament—Sacred Heart of Jesus—Sacred Heart of Mary—Immaculate Conception—Holy Name of Mary—Our Lady of Prompt Succor—Holy Angels— Angel Guardian—St. Joseph—St. Mary Magdalen—St. Patrick—St. Bridget—St. Francis of Assisi—St. Ignatius—St. Francis Xavier—St. Aloysius—St. Stanislaus —St. Teresa—St. Francis de Sales—St. Jane de Chantal—St. Vincent de Paul—St. Alphonsus Liguori—Litany of Providence—of the Faithful Departed—of a Good Intention—of the Will of God—Golden Litany, &c., &c.
No Prayer Book in the language contains a greater number of Prayers, drawn from the works of Canonized Saints and Ascetical Writers, approved by the Church.

PRICE.

American morocco, embossed, 1 plate $1 00
"          "          marbled edge,
                    1 plate,   1 25
Arabesque     "      gilt edges, 1 plate,   1 75
American       "       "       "   5 plates,  2 25
Imitation Turkey, gilt sides & edges,
    5 plates,   .   .   .   .   .   2 50
Turkey morocco,   .   .   .   .   3 00
"          "      super extra, 14 plates, 3 50
"          "      antique, bevell'd, 14
                    plates, 4 00

Turkey morocco, rim & clasp, embossed edges, 14 plates, $5 00
"          "      Venetian style, 14
                    plates, 5 50
Velvet, rim and clasps, 14 plates,   .   7 50
"      rim, clasps and corners, 9 to 12 00
"      "    full ornaments,   10 to 15 00
"      "    and clasp with medallion,
            ivory or cameo, 14 plates, 20 00
"  full ivory or tortoise shell side,
            clasp,   .   .   .   .   25 00

## APPROBATION OF THE ORDINARY.
*
"St. John's Manual," having been duly examined, we hereby approve of its publication.

✠ JOHN, Archbishop of New York.

New York, Aug. 25, 1856.

3*

58

*Archbishop Blanc of New Orleans.*

"St. John's Manual" is, beyond all contradiction, the most complete collection of all that, in the way of prayers and exercises of devotion, can best aid to follow profitably the public service of the Church in this Country, and to nourish private piety and devotion. I shall be most happy if my commendation induces the Catholics of my diocese who speak English to obtain it.

Yours devotedly in Xt.,

✠ ANTH., **Archbishop of New Orleans.**

*Archbishop of Quebec.*

It is an excellent book, and cannot fail to increase sentiments of devotion in those who have it in their possession. May it be circulated among the faithful.

✠ P. F., **Archbishop of Quebec.**

*Bishop Timon of Buffalo.*

A good manual of prayer is of great advantage to the Catholic public. Such, we think, is the "St. John's Manual," published by Messrs. Dunigan & Brother, with the approbation of the Most Rev. Dr. Hughes. At the request of the publishers we cheerfully recommend it to the faithful.

✠ JOHN, **Bishop of Buffalo.**

Feast of the Immaculate Conception, 8th Dec., 1856.

*Bishop Loughlin of Brooklyn.*

We most cheerfully recommend the "St. John's Manual," approved by the Most Rev. Dr. Hughes.

✠ JOHN, Bishop of Brooklyn.
✠ ANDREW, Bishop of Little Rock.

Brooklyn, Dec. 10, 1856.

*Bishop McCloskey of Albany.*

I fully approve of and recommend the prayer-book entitled "St. John's Manual," and published by Dunigan & Brother.

✠ JOHN, Bishop of Albany.

*Bishop Young of Erie.*

Your "St. John's Manual" is certainly the most comprehensive and complete prayer book that I have met with in the English language, while its various instructions and devotions seem admirably adapted to guide and, I would hope, stimulate the piety of the faithful. Your enterprise, in bringing it out so neatly and so sumptuously, will, therefore, be a success entirely well deserved, on which I congratulate you.

✠ J. M. YOUNG, Bishop of Erie.

*Bishop Bacon of Portland.*

It is unnecessary to ask my approval of a prayer-book to the Catholic public with the approbation of our most venerated and Rev. Archbishop. I have, however, examined the work since the reception of a copy, and think it most appropriate to the use of the faithful. I offer you my congratulations on your enterprise and zeal, and pray that you may be ever successful and reap a rich harvest in return.

✠ DAVID W., Bishop of Portland

*Bishop Spalding of Louisville.*

Having examined the prayer-book, "The St. John's Manual," lately published by Dunigan & Brother, we take pleasure in uniting with the Most Rev. Archbishop of New York, in approving the same, and in recommending it to the faithful of our diocese.

✠ MARTIN JOHN SPALDING, Bishop of Louisville.

# 59

*Bishop Connolly of St. John.*

Your truly splendid "St. John's Manual" is quite equal, if not superior, to any thing of the kind I have seen in the old country, and must be, I am sure, all that could suit the taste of the fastidious at this side of the Atlantic.

✠ THOMAS L. CONNOLLY, Bishop of St. John.

---

*Bishop Henni of Milwaukee.*

Aside from its truly handsome mechanical execution, well worthy of your firm, "St. John's Manual" is a well-selected and complete compendium of devotion for a great portion of our people. May they profit by your noble endeavor, for such is the wish of

Yours, truly devoted,

✠ JOHN MARTIN, Bishop of Milwaukee.

Feb. 22d, 1857.

---

*Bishop Bourget of Montreal.*

Having examined a new prayer-book, entitled "St. John's Manual," published by the house of Dunigan & Brother, New York, we approve it by these presents, and recommend it to the piety of the faithful.

✠ I. G., Bishop of Montreal.

Montreal, Feb. 27th, 1857.

---

*Bishop Demers of Vancouver's Island.*

I am very happy to avail myself of this opportunity to add my humble approbation to that already given the "St. John's Manual," by many Archbishops and Bishops of this country. . . . . Among the many works of piety offered to the Catholic community, I have no hesitation in saying that "St. John's Manual" deserves an eminent rank.

✠ MOD. DEMERS, Bishop of Vancouver's Island.

June, 1857.

---

*Bishop Miles of Nashville.*

I highly approve of the "St. John's Manual," and recommend it to the Catholics of my diocese and all others of the United States.

✠ RICHARD PIUS MILES, Bishop of Nashville.

Nashville, March 4, 1857.

---

*Bishop Martin of Natchitoches.*

I already knew this excellent book from the unanimous commendations of our Catholic papers, but I must acknowledge I had no correct idea of its high merit and value.

"St. John's Manual" is certainly, in every respect, superior to any prayer-book ever published in this country, nor do I know of any one in Europe so complete in what is usual, and so rich in precious selections.

Receive my share of gratitude, as a Bishop, for your persevering endeavors to make yourself useful to our Holy Church.

✠ AUG., Bishop of Natchitoches.

Natchitoches, March 3, 1857.

---

*Bishop Larocque of Cydonia.*

"St. John's Manual," having been carefully examined by his Grace, the Archbishop of New York, I cannot but have every confidence in its perfect orthodoxy. The approbation which you ask of me can refer only to its utility. In this respect, I do but simple justice in awarding my praise to the judicious and pious discernment with which the author has compiled the many prayers and instructions condensed in this collection. May "St. John's Manual" find its way to every family, it will meet every want, satisfy every desire as a book of devotion.

✠ JOS., Bishop of Cydonia.

St. Hyacinthe, 9th March, 1857.

*Bishop McGill of Richmond.*

An examination of the table of contents and the general plan of your new prayer-book, the "St. John's Manual," satisfies me that it is a very useful and elegant book of devotion. It seems to be at once comprehensive and complete, containing valuable instructions concerning the sacraments and other matters of Christian practice, and offering most beautiful prayers and appropriate exercises for the different devotions and pious associations, which the Church approves as aids to a spiritual life.

✠ John McGill, Bishop of Richmond.

*Bishop Blanchet of Nesqualy.*

The approbation of the Most Rev. Archbishop of New York is, doubtless, sufficient to attest the usefulness and value of "St. John's Manual." Yet I cannot withhold my humble approbation, which I willingly add to that of the illustrious prelate.

Augustine M. Al., Bishop of Nesqualy.
Washington Territory, May 21, 1857.

*Bishop Baraga of Saut Sainte Marie.*

After a due examination of "St. John's Manual," published by Messrs. Ed. Dunigan & Brother (James B. Kirker), New York, I find that it is the most complete and perfect prayer-book that ever has come to my knowledge, not only in English but also in several other languages. It is a new proof of the old assertion, that the Catholic community of the United States are under great obligations to Dunigan & Brother's old publishing establishment, for the compilation and publication of useful Catholic works.

✠ Frederic Baraga, Bishop of Saut Sainte Marie.
June 1, 1857.

NOTICES OF THE PRESS.

"This is a new, and we think will be a formidable aspirant to popularity among the host of prayer-books now in favor. 'St. John's Manual' is a fresh compilation, and avoids the absurdity to be found in many other prayer-books, of offices peculiar to other countries, and unmeaningly reprinted here. It is enough for the elegance of the book to say, that Dunigan & Brother have gotten it up in their best style. It is a very complete manual, and possesses many merits not shared with other prayer-books."—*Freeman's Journal.*

"We thought there was an end of prayer-book making progress. But 'St. John's Manual,' just published by Dunigan & Brother, surpasses all its predecessors. It contains the ordinary of the Mass, Epistles and Gospels for all the festivals of the year, Devotions, Litanies, Novenas, &c., in a more convenient form—just the thing to take the eye and satisfy the devout."—*Catholic Telegraph and Advocate.*

"This is a new prayer-book, got up expressly for the wants of the present time, and adapted to the use of the faithful in this country; the Office Books and Rituals, authorized for use in the United States, being strictly followed. It is the most complete prayer-book that has been issued from the Catholic press of this country, and will, we feel confident, become the favorite of the faithful."—*Pittsburg Catholic.*

"This is one of the most beautiful of the many fine editions of Catholic prayer-books issued by this house. There are some fifteen beautifully executed engravings, and the style of printing and designs ornamental, are in good and appropriate taste. As a prayer-book, 'St. John's Manual' is destined to become a favorite. The devotional prayers are in large print, which is very desirable. There are no less than forty-seven Litanies to be found, and the other exercises are proportionately numerous."—*Leader.*

"This is certainly the most complete collection of devotional exercises that has yet been published."—*Catholic Herald.*

"We are very late in noticing this excellent Manual, which has been before the public nearly two years. Although it contains several Litanies not approved by the Church, as do nearly all our Manuals, it is, to our judgment and taste, one of the very best of the 'monster' prayer-books that have been published. We are not, for ourselves, in favor of such huge prayer-books, .... but, if we must have them, we think the one before us is the very best."—*Brownson's Review.* (Jan. 1858.)

# I. BIBLES AND TESTAMENTS.

PUBLISHED UNDER THE APPROBATION OF THE

## MOST REV. JOHN HUGHES, ARCHBISHOP OF NEW YORK.

### DUNIGAN & BROTHER'S

*New, cheap, superbly illustrated, and unabridged edition of*

### Haydock's Catholic Family Bible and Commentary,

THE MOST COMPREHENSIVE IN THE ENGLISH LANGUAGE.

THE HOLY BIBLE, translated from the Latin Vulgate, diligently compared with the Hebrew, Greek, and other Editions in various languages. The OLD TESTAMENT, first published by the English College at Douay, A.D. 1609; and the NEW TESTAMENT, first published by the English College at Rheims, A.D. 1582, with useful-Notes, Critical, Historical, Controversial, and Explanatory, from the most eminent Commentators, and able and judicious critics.

#### BY THE REV. GEO. LEO HAYDOCK, D.D.

Splendidly embellished by eminent Artists, after the great Masters. This Edition contains in full the many thousand Critical, Explanatory, and Practical Notes, illustrative of the Text, with References, Readings, Chronological Tables; and Indexes of the great Original Work, being an exact reprint of the Edition approved of by the Catholic Hierarchy in England and Ireland. It is published under the approbation of the MOST REV. JOHN HUGHES, D.D., Archbishop of New York, and more than thirty of the Archbishops and Bishops of the United States and Canadas.

PRICE—American morocco, embossed, . . . . . . $14
     Turkey    "    gilt edges, . . . . . . . . 16
      "     "    super extra gilt edges . . . . . . 18
      "     "    bevelled . . . . . . . . 20
      "     "    panelled sides, . . . . . . . 25

Also in 38 parts, at 25 cents a part.

### Approbation of the Ordinary.

"This new edition of the English version of the Bible, with the complete notes of Bishop Challoner, Rev. Geo. Leo Haydock, and others, known as Haydock's Catholic Bible, having been duly examined, we hereby approve of its republication by Edward Dunigan and Brother, of this city.

"Given at New York, this 5th day of May, 1852, under our hand and seal,

"✠ JOHN, ARCHBISHOP OF NEW YORK

#### APPROVED ALSO BY

Cardinal *Wiseman*, Archbishops *Romily*, of Milan, *Claret*, of Cuba; *F. P. Kenrick*, of Baltimore ; *Purcell*, of Cincinnati ; *P. R. Kenrick*, of St. Louis ; and *Alemany*, of San Francisco ; Bishops *Bacon*, of Portland ; *De Goesbriand*, of Burlington ; *Fitzpatrick*, of Boston ; *Loughlin*, of Brooklyn ; *McCloskey*, of Albany ; *Timon*, of Buffalo ; *Bayley*, of Newark ; *O'Connor*, of Pittsburg ; *Young*, of Erie ; *Whelan*, of Wheeling ; *Reynolds*, of Charleston ; *Portier*, of Mobile ; *Vandevelde*, of Natchez ; *Odin*, of Galveston ; *Rappe*, of Cleveland ; *De St. Palais*, of Vincennes ; *O'Regan*, of Chicago ; *Lefevee*, of Detroit ; *Baraga*, of Upper Michigan ; *Henni*, of Milwaukie ; *Loras*, of Dubuque ; *Cretin*, of St. Paul's ; *Spalding*, of Louisville ; *Miles*, of Nashville ; *Blanchet*, of Nesqualy ; *Charbonnel*, of Toronto ; *Demers*, of Vancouver's Island ; *Menyaud*, of Nancy, &c., &c.

**DOUAY BIBLE.** Illustrated Family Edition. Imperial 8vo. Printed in double columns, with parallel References, Illuminated Title, Family Records, and many exquisite Engravings from the great Masters.

PRICE—Superb Turkey morocco, 15 illustrations, . . . . . . . $9 00
American morocco, ill. gilt sides and edges, 14 Ills. . . . 5 00
" " gilt edges, 14 Illustrations, . . . . 4 50
Embossed " fancy edges, 14 Illustrations, . . . 8 00

**CHEAP EDITION.—**Royal Octavo.
American morocco, illuminated, gilt sides and edges, . . $4 00
" " full gilt sides and edges, 6 Illustrations, . 3 50
" " gilt edges, 6 Illustrations, . . . . 8 00
" " gilt back and sides, fancy edges, . . . 2 50
Embossed " gilt back, fancy edges, 4 plates, . . . 2 00
Sheep bindings, 1 plate, . . . . . . . . 1 50

**THE NEW TESTAMENT OF OUR LORD AND SAVIOUR JESUS CHRIST.** Translated from the Latin Vulgate, and first published by the English College at Rheims, A.D. 1582, with Annotations, a Chronological Index, Table of References, &c., &c. Neat 12mo.—Cloth, plain, . . . . . . . $0 81
Gilt edges, . . . . . . . 0 75

**EL NUEVO TESTAMENTO DE NUESTRO SENOR I SALVADOR JESU CRISTO.** Nuevamente traducido por el exmo. Sr. Don Felix Torres Amat, Obispo de Astorga. Lleva algunas notas tomadas del P. Scio i otras calificados interpretes—con la aprobacion del ilmo. FR. JOSE S. ALEMANY, Arzobispo de San Franciso. A cheap and accurate edition of the approved Spanish translation.
PRICE—Cloth, plain, . . . . . . . . . . . $1 00
American morocco, . . . . . . . . . . 1 25
Turkey morocco, . . . . . . . . . . 2 50

**THE ACTS OF THE APOSTLES, THE EPISTLES OF ST. PAUL, THE CATHOLIC EPISTLES, AND THE APOCALYPSE.** 8vo. Uniform with the "Four Gospels." With Notes, Critical and Explanatory. By the MOST REV. FRANCIS PATRICK KENRICK, D.D., Archbishop of Baltimore.
This volume completes Archbishop Kenrick's version of the New Testament. It is invaluable to the clergy, and all who study the sacred volume.
PRICE—Cloth, . . . . . . . . . . . . . $2 50

---

# II. PRAYER BOOKS, BOOKS OF DEVOTION, AND HYMN BOOKS.

PUBLISHED UNDER THE APPROBATION OF THE

## MOST REV. JOHN HUGHES, D.D., ARCHBISHOP OF NEW YORK.

## EDWARD DUNIGAN & BROTHER,

THE LARGEST ASSORTMENT OF

# STANDARD CATHOLIC PRAYER BOOKS,

In the English, French, German, and Spanish Languages,

ALL NEW AND BEAUTIFUL EDITIONS,

*In various sizes, and in every variety of Cheap and Elegant Bindings.*

They call especial attention to their beautiful presentation editions in velvet, with silver, tortoise shell, ivory, and medallion ornaments, which are unsurpassed for beauty by any works in the country.

**ST. JOHN'S MANUAL.** See previous pages.

**URSULINE MANUAL.** New and superb edition, 864 pages. Illustrated with a beautiful Illuminated Presentation Page, and Twelve Illustrations of the highest finish and beauty, after Overbeck, Carlo Dolci, Sassoferrato, and others.

| | |
|---|---|
| Fine Ed., 32mo.—Velvet, full ornaments, 18 fine plates, | $3 50 |
| " clasps and corners, 18 plates, | 6 00 |
| " embossed, with clasp, 18 plates, | 4 50 |
| Turkey morocco, super extra gilt edges, with clasp, 18 plates, | 3 00 |
| " " " " with 18 plates, | 2 50 |
| " " gilt edges, 10 plates, | 2 00 |
| American " " 10 plates, | 1 50 |
| Cheap Ed.—American morocco, full gilt sides and clasp, 10 plates, | 1 50 |
| " gilt sides and edges, with 6 plates, | 1 00 |
| Roan " gilt edges, 2 plates, | 0 75 |
| " " gilt back, 1 plate, | 0 50 |

**CATHOLIC PIETY.** By the Rev. WILLIAM GAHAN, O.S A. Newly revised, corrected, and greatly enlarged by a Catholic priest. Large type, 768 pages, 24mo. An Illuminated Presentation Page, and 10 of the fine Engravings, from Overbeck, &c.

| | |
|---|---|
| PRICE—Velvet, full ornaments, illuminated presentation page, and 10 splendidly engraved plates, | $6 50 |
| Velvet, clasps and corners, 11 plates, | 4 50 |
| " embossed, with clasp, 11 plates, | 8 50 |
| Turkey morocco, sup. ext. gilt edges and clasp, 11 plates, | 8 38 |
| " " super extra gilt edges, 11 plates | 2 00 |
| " " gilt edges, 10 plates, | 1 50 |
| American " gilt edges, with clasps, 10 plates, | 1 00 |
| American mor., full gilt edges and sides, with clasp, 7 plates, | 0 88 |
| American morocco, illuminated sides, gilt edges, | 0 88 |
| " " full gilt sides and edges, 7 plates, | 0 75 |
| American moroc., gilt sides and edges, 7 plates, | 0 68 |
| " " gilt sides, 2 plates, | 0 50 |
| Roan morocco, gilt back, 1 plate, | 0 38 |

**THE MISSION BOOK.** A Manual of Instruction and Prayer, adapted to preserve the Fruit of the Mission. Drawn chiefly from the Works of ST. ALPHONSUS LIGUORI, published under the direction of the Fathers of the Congregation of the Most Holy Redeemer.

| | |
|---|---|
| 18mo.—Neat sheep binding, | $0 50 |
| American morocco, gilt sides and back, | 0 75 |
| " " gilt edges | 1 00 |
| Turkey morocco, | 2 25 |
| 24mo.—Neat Roan, | |
| American morocco, gilt sides and back, | |
| " " gilt edges, | |
| Turkey, | |

**FLOWERS OF PIETY.** THE GEM OF PRAYER-BOOKS. New large type, and elegant edition of this most comprehensive and beautiful Prayer-book; with a splendid illuminated presentation page, and 10 fine engraved Illustrations, by the first artists in America, from designs of Overbeck, Steinle, and other great painters.

| | |
|---|---|
| PRICE.—Velvet, various exquisite styles, | from $4 to $6 00 |
| Velvet, clasps and corners, 10 plates, | 4 00 |
| Turkey morocco, super extra gilt edges, clasp, 10 plates. | 2 25 |
| " " super extra gilt edges, 10 plates, | 1 75 |
| Cheap Ed., 32mo.—American morocco, gilt edges and clasp, 8 plates, | 0 68 |
| " " " illuminated sides, | 0 68 |
| " " " 8 plates, | 0 50 |
| " " gilt sides, 4 plates, | 0 38 |
| Roan morocco, gilt back, 1 plate, | 0 25 |
| Cheap Ed., 48mo.—American morocco, gilt edges and clasp, 8 plates, | 0 68 |
| " " " 8 plates, | 0 50 |
| " " gilt back and sides, 1 plate, | 0 31 |
| Sheep. | 0 19 |

**LITTLE FLOWERS OF PIETY.** Gentlemen's vest-pocket edition.

| | |
|---|---|
| PRICE.—Embossed morocco, | 0 38 |
| Turkey flexible, | 0 75 |

64

**DEVOUT MANUAL.**
It is beautifully printed on a large open type, and is believed to be the most useful, the cheapest, and most elegant Prayer-book printed.

PRICE.—Turkey morocco, super extra gilt edges, 8 plates, . . . $1 50
    "    "    full gilt, clasp, 8 plates, . . . . 1 75
    American morocco, full gilt sides and edges, clasps, 8 plates, . 0 63
    "    "    illum. sides, gilt edges, 8 plates, . . 0 63
    "    "    full gilt sides and edges, 8 plates, . . 0 50
    "    "    gilt sides, 2 plates, . . . . ( 88
    Roan Morocco, gilt back, 1 plate, . . . . . 0 25
Devout Manual, edition for the aged, 18mo., plates.

PRICE.—Turkey, super extra, clasp, . . . . . . 3 00
    Turkey, extra, . . . . . . . . 2 50
    American morocco, gilt edges and sides, . . . . 1 50
    "    "    gilt edges, . . . . . . 1 00
    "    "    gilt sides, . . . . . . 0 73
    Roan, . . . . . . . . 0 50

**DAILY PIETY.** A Guide to Catholic Devotions; for general use. With thirty-six Pictorial Illustrations, selections of the best Litanies, Hymns, &c.

PRICE.—Turkey morocco, super extra, 8 plates, . . . $1 50
    "    "    full gilt sides and edg., clasps, 8 plates, . 1 75
    American morocco, full gilt sides and edges, clasps, 8 plates, . 0 63
    "    "    illuminated sides, gilt edges, 8 plates, . 0 63
    "    "    full gilt sides and edges, . . . 0 50
    "    "    gilt back and sides, . . . . 0 38
    Roan, gilt back, . . . . . . . 0 25
    Handsome cloth binding, . . . . . . 0 19

**THE SERAPHIC MANUAL.** A selection of Devotions according to the spirit of the Catholic Church, with the Rule of the Third Order of St. Francis: Confraternity of the Cord, &c., 24mo., price, . . . . . . . 50 cents to 2 00

**KEY OF HEAVEN.** 24mo.
PRICE.—Turkey morocco, sup. extra gilt edges and clasp, 9 plates, . $2 25
    "    "    super extra gilt edges, 9 plates, . . . 1 75
    American morocco, gilt edges and clasp, 6 plates, . . 0 88
    "    "    "    illuminated sides, . . . 0 88
    "    "    "    6 plates, . . . . 0 75
    "    "    "    4 plates, . . . . 0 68
    "    "    gilt sides, 2 plates, . . . . 0 50
    Roan morocco, gilt back, 1 plate, . . . . 0 38

**CHILD'S CATHOLIC PIETY.** New, cheap, and beautiful Child's Prayer-book. 384 pages. 48mo. From 19 cents to $1 25. Numerous fine wood illustrations.
PRICE—Turkey morocco, super extra, 8 plates, . . . $1 38
    American morocco, or cloth, gilt edges, 8 plates, . . 0 38
    Cloth, gilt sides and back, 4 plates, . . . . 0 25
    Handsome cloth binding, 1 plate, . . . . . 0 19

**CATHOLIC'S POCKET COMPANION.** A well-known pocket manual. 254 pp.
PRICE—Cloth, plain edges, . . . . . . . $0 19
    Roan, gilt back, . . . . . . . 0 20
    American morocco, gilt back and sides, . . . . 0 31
    "    "    full gilt sides and edges, . . . 0 38
    "    "    tuck, . . . . . 0 38

**POCKET CATHOLIC MANUAL.** Smallest size Prayer-book printed: with beautiful wood illustrations, and plain type. 64mo.
PRICE.—Cloth, plain edges, . . . . . . . $0 12
    "    gilt back, . . . . . . 0 19
    "    gilt edges, 2 plates, . . . . . 0 25
    Turkey morocco, extra, 6 plates, . . . . . 0 75

**MASS AND VESPER BOOK.** A Pocket Prayer for Mass and Vespers, in large type. 64mo.
PRICE—Cloth, . . . . . . . . $0 13
    Gilt edges, 2 plates, . . . . . . . 0 25
    Turkey morocco, extra, 6 plates, . . . . . 0 75

**Das Paradies Gärtlein.** New German Prayer, with 36 Illustrations of the Mass. Containing the most indispensable Prayers and Exercises of Devotions, with beautiful Litanies, Hymns, &c. 32mo.

PRICE—Roan morocco, gilt back, . . . . . . . . $0 25
    American morocco, gilt sides, . . . . . . . 0 38
    " " full gilt sides and edges, . . . . 0 50
    " " " clasp, . . . 0 63
    " " illuminated sides, gilt edges, . . . 0 63
    Turkey morocco, gilt sides and edges, . . . . 1 50
**Berg Zum Himmel.** New German Prayer and Hymn Book. 24mo., 608 pages.
PRICE—Roan morocco, gilt back, . . . . . . . 0 38
    Imitation morocco, plain edges, . . . . . 0 50
    " " gilt edges, . . . . . . 0 75
    American morocco, gilt edges and clasp, . . . . 0 88
    " " illuminated sides, . . . . . 0 88
    Turkey morocco, gilt edges, . . . . . . 1 75

## L'ANGE CONDUCTEUR.
This new and beautiful French Prayer-book is considered one of the best and most complete Prayer-books published, containing in fact almost every thing required. 674 pages. 24mo.
PRICE—Rich velvet, various splendid styles, . . . from $6 to $8 00
    Turkey mor., sup. ex. gilt edges and clasp, 9 plates, . . . 2 25
    " " super extra, gilt edges, 9 plates, . . . . 2 00
    " " gilt edges, 8 plates, . . . . . 1 50
    American morocco, gilt edges and clasp, 6 plates, . . . 0 88
    " " gilt edges, 6 plates, . . . . . 0 75
    " " gilt edges, 4 plates, . . . . . 0 63
    " " gilt sides, 2 plates, . . . . . 0 50
    Roan morocco, 1 plate, . . . . . . . . 0 38

## EL DIAMANTE DEL AMERICANO CATOLICO.
This beautiful Spanish Prayer-book has been pronounced by eminent judges as the most comprehensive and best Spanish Prayer-book ever printed,
Published with the approbation of Right Rev. Fr. S. Alemany, Bishop of Monterey in California. With 86 wood-cut Illustrations of the Holy Sacrifice of the Mass, and 9 fine steel Illustrations.
PRICE—Rich velvet, several elegant patterns, . . . from $6 to $8 00
    Turkey mor., sup. ex. gilt edges and clasp, 9 plates, . . 2 25
    " " super extra, gilt edges, 9 plates, . . . . 2 00
    " " gilt edges and sides, 8 plates, . . . . 1 50
    American morocco, gilt edges and sides, and clasp, 9 plates, . 1 18
    " " gilt edges and sides, . . . . . 1 00
    " " gilt sides, 4 plates, . . . . . 0 75
    Roan morocco, 1 plate, . . . . . . . . 0 50

## THE GOLDEN BOOK OF THE CONFRATERNITIES, Adapted to the
Rosary, Living Rosary, Scapular Societies, Confraternities of the Blessed Sacrament, Sacred Heart of Jesus, Immaculate Heart of Mary. Cord of St. Francis, &c., &c., with Prayers for Mass and Vespers, Way of the Cross, &c.
PRICE—One vol. neat cloth, . . . . . . . . . 0 38

## THE SERAPHIC STAFF.
A Manual for the Members of the Third Order of St. Francis Seraph, compiled for the accommodation of those living in America by a Priest of the Order of St. Francis. 32mo.
PRICE—Neat cloth, . . . . . . . . . . $0 19

## EXERCISE OF THE WAY OF THE CROSS, As it is performed at Jerusalem
and in the Colosseum at Rome. Translated from the Italian by a Priest of the Order of St. Francis. 32mo.
PRICE—Paper, 4 cents.
Exercise of the Way of the Cross, by St. Alphonsus Liguori, with engravings of the Passion, 32mo. PRICE 4 cents.
Via Crucis or the Holy Way of the Cross, by Abp. Walsh. 6¼ cents.

## THE ROSARY OF THE BLESSED VIRGIN MARY.
This is the first complete Rosary Manual published in this country. Besides the usual explanation of the Mysteries and appropriate Prayers, it contains various methods of reciting the Beads, especially that used in the Redemptorist Mission, and an explanation and the Rules of the Living Rosary.
The Engravings are new, highly finished, and got up expressly for this work.
PRICE—Paper covers, 6 cents.

**THE SCAPULAR BOOK.** Containing a full explanation of the Scapular of Mount Carmel, the advantages of that excellent devotion, and a list of the Indulgences to be gained by its use. Besides this the reader will find in it the devotions of five other Scapulars approved by the Holy See and enriched by the grant of indulgences.

**EUCHARISTICA ; OR, A SERIES OF PIECES, ORIGINAL AND TRANS-LATED, ON THE MOST HOLY AND ADORABLE SACRAMENT OF THE EUCHARIST.** By Arbp. Walsh. PRICE—1 vol. neat clo. 68 cts.

**LENTEN MANUAL, AND COMPANION FOR PASSION TIME AND HOLY WEEK.** Translated and compiled from various sources. 476 pages, 24mo.
PRICE—Cloth, 87½ cents.

**STATIONS FOR THE HOLY TIME OF LENT.** From the French of Père Berthier, S. J. PRICE—6¼ cents.

**SEVEN WORDS OF JESUS ON THE CROSS.** PRICE—6¼ cents.

**EXPOSITION OF THE LAMENTATIONS OF THE PROPHET JERE-MIAH.** PRICE—12½ cents.

**THE REAL PRESENCE OF JESUS CHRIST IN THE MOST HOLY EUCHARIST.** 18mo. PRICE—12½ cents.

**THE LOVING TESTAMENT OF JESUS.** 18mo. PRICE—9 cents.

**PURGATORY OPENED** to the Piety of the Faithful, or the Month of November, consecrated to the Relief of the Souls in Purgatory.
PRICE.—Neat cloth binding, 31 cents.

**LYRA CATHOLICA.** The most comprehensive and elegant Catholic Hymn-book printed in the English Language.

| | | |
|---|---|---|
| PRICE.—Superb Turkey morocco, fine frontispiece, 16mo. | | $2 00 |
| Fine cloth, gilt edges, 16mo. | | 1 00 |
| Cloth, gilt edges, 24mo. | | 0 75 |
| Handsomely bound in cloth, | | 0 50 |

**CATHOLIC HYMN BOOK.** Containing a collection of Hymns, Anthems, &c., for all the Holy Days of Obligation and Devotion throughout the year. 32mo.

| | | |
|---|---|---|
| PRICE—Cloth, | | $0 25 |
| American morocco, | | 0 38 |
| "          gilt, | | 0 50 |
| Superb Turkey morocco, | | 1 50 |

**LITTLE CATHOLIC HYMN-BOOK.** Principally designed for Sunday Schools. 32mo.

| | | |
|---|---|---|
| PRICE—Paper, | | $0 06 |
| Cloth, | | 0 19 |
| "     gilt edges, | | 0 31 |

**CATHOLIC CHORALIST.** Containing a selection of Catholic Hymns, Psalms, and Litanies, set to music, being the cheapest Catholic music book published. 24mo.

| | | |
|---|---|---|
| PRICE—Neat paper binding, | | $0 09 |
| Half bound | | 0 10 |

**Katholisches Gesangbuch.** A new German Hymn Book.

| | | |
|---|---|---|
| PRICE—Paper | | 0 09 |
| Neat cloth, gilt | | 0 19 |

---

# III. CATECHISMS.

**THE DOCTRINAL CATECHISM.** Being a new and enlarged edition of Scheff-macher's Controversial Catechism. By the Rev. STEPHEN KEENAN.

| | | |
|---|---|---|
| PRICE—Fancy paper | | $0 25 |
| Half cloth | | 0 31¼ |
| Fine paper, cloth. | | 0 50 |

**THE POOR MAN'S CATECHISM ;** or, The Christian Doctrine Explained, with short admonitions, by FATHER JOHN MANNOCK, of the Order of St. Benedict.

| | | |
|---|---|---|
| PRICE—Paper | | $0 19 |
| Cloth | | 0 38 |

**THE DOUAY CATECHISM ;** or, an Abridgment of the Christian Doctrine. With proofs on points controverted, by way of question and answer. Composed, in 1649, by the Rev. HENRY TUBERVILLE, D.D.

| | | |
|---|---|---|
| PRICE—Paper binding | | $0 13 |
| Half bound | | 0 19 |

**BUTLER'S CATECHISM.** Revised, enlarged, improved, and printed in large type. 18mo. By the Most Rev. JAMES BUTLER. PRICE—6¼ cents.
**THE CATECHISM;** or, a short Abridgment of the Christian Doctrine. 32mo, PRICE—3 cents.
**EL CATECISMO DE LA DOCTRINA CRISTIANA.** Por el P. RIPALDA, Corregido y aumentado, para el uso de la Diocesi de Monterey, California. PRICE—6¼ cents. $4 per hundred.
**EL NUEVO CATON CRISTIANO.** " 10 " 6 " "
**EL CATECISMO DE LA DOCTRINA CRISTIANA DEL PADRE ASTETE.** Illustrated. . . . . . . . PRICE—10 cents. $6 per hundred.

---

# IV. CONTROVERSIAL WORKS.

**BROOKSIANA;** or, the Controversy between Senator Brooks and Archbishop Hughes, growing out of the recently enacted Church Property Bill, with an Introduction by the Most Rev. Archbishop of New York.
PRICE—1 vol. paper, . . . . . . . . . 20 cents.
Half bound . . . . . . . . . 25 "
Cloth . . . . . . . . . 38 "
**KIRWAN UNMASKED.** A Review of Kirwan, in Six Letters. Addressed to the Rev. Nicholas Murray, D.D.. of Elizabethtown, by the Most Rev. JOHN HUGHES, D.D., Archbishop of New York.
PRICE—6¼ cents, or 50 cents per dozen.
**ASPIRATIONS OF NATURE.** By I. T. HECKER, Author of the Questions of the Soul. PRICE—Cloth, 12mo. . . . . . . . . 75 cents.
**THE MANUAL OF CONTROVERSY.** Containing in one volume, 16mo. size, the celebrated works of the Grounds of the Catholic Doctrine ; the Papist Misrepresented and Truly Represented ; and Fifty Reasons why the Roman Catholic Religion ought to be Preferred to all others.
PRICE—Cloth binding . . . . . . 50 cents.
**THE GROUNDS OF THE CATHOLIC DOCTRINE,** Contained in the Profession of Faith published by Pope Pius IV., to which are added Reasons why a Catholic cannot conform to the Protestant Religion.
PRICE—Neat paper binding, 9 cents. Per doz. . . . . $0 75
Cloth . . . 18¾ cts. " . . . . 1 50
**FIFTY REASONS WHY THE ROMAN CATHOLIC RELIGION OUGHT TO BE PREFERRED TO ALL OTHERS.** By ANTHONY ULRIC, Duke of Brunswick and Lunenburg, a Convert from Lutheranism.
PRICE—Neat paper binding, 9 cents. Per doz. . . . . $0 75
Cloth . . 18¾ cts. " . . . . 1 50
**THE PAPIST MISREPRESENTED. AND TRULY REPRESENTED;** Or, A TWOFOLD CHARACTER OF POPERY. By Rev. JOHN GOTHER.
PRICE—Neat paper binding, 9 cents. Per doz. . . . $0 75
Cloth, . . .18¾ cts. . . . 1 50
**MILNER'S END OF RELIGIOUS CONTROVERSY.** Printed from the last edition, revised by the author. 1 vol. 12mo. With the Apostolical Tree.
PRICE—Neat paper covers, . . . . . . . 25 cents.
Sheep and cloth binding, . . . . . . 50 cents.
**THE CLIFTON TRACTS.** Published with the approbation of Cardinal Wiseman. 4 vols. 12mo. PRICE—33 cents per volume.
**THE CHURCH AND THE BIBLE, HOW ARE THEY RELATED TO EACH OTHER?** 1 neat vol., cloth, 18 cents.
**PROTESTANTISM WEIGHED IN ITS OWN BALANCE AND FOUND WANTING.** 1 vol. flexible cloth, 19 cents.
**QUESTIONS TO A PROTESTANT FRIEND.** 1 vol. neat cloth, 19 cents.
**CATHOLIC FESTIVALS AND DEVOTIONS.** 1 vol. neat cloth, 19 cents.
**HOW THE POPES OBTAINED THEIR TEMPORAL POWER.** 1 vol. flexible cloth, 19 cents.
**THE MASS AND CEREMONIES OF THE CATHOLIC CHURCH EXPLAINED.** 1 vol. flexible cloth, 19 cents.

**SURE WAY TO FIND OUT THE TRUE RELIGION.**
PRICE—One volume, paper binding, . . . . . . 12½ cents
    Cloth, . . . . . . . . . . . . 19 "
**DEFENSA DE ALGUNOS PUNTOS DE LA DOCTRINA CATOLICA,**
Aprobada por el Revmo. Fr. Sadoc Alemani, Abpo. de San Francisco.
PRICE—Paper, . . . . . . . . . . . . 88 cents.

# . DEVOTIONAL WORKS.

### PUBLISHED UNDER THE APPROBATION OF

## THE MOST REV. JOHN HUGHES, D.D.,

#### ARCHBISHOP OF NEW YORK.

*Beautiful Gift-Book for all Seasons.*

**THE CATHOLIC OFFERING.** By the Most Rev. WM. WALSH, D.D., Archbishop of Halifax.
An elegant description of the great festivals and devotions of the Christian year, beautifully printed, and illustrated with rich illuminations and fine steel engravings.
PRICE—Turkey morocco, gilt edges. 13 plates, . . . . $3 00
    Beautiful cloth, gilt edges. 13 plates, . . . . . 2 50
    Cloth, gilt edges, with 8 plates, . . . . . . 2 00
    Cloth, plain edges, with 5 plates, . . . . . 1 50

**THE PRACTICE OF CHRISTIAN AND RELIGIOUS PERFECTION.**
By ALPHONSUS RODRIGUEZ, of the Society of Jesus. This invaluable work, the treasure of Seminaries, and religious houses of every order, so justly styled the "daily bread" of the novice in the ways of perfection, is not less valuable for every Christian family. 3 volumes, 8vo. PRICE—$2 50

**THE FOLLOWING OF CHRIST.** 32mo., cheap edition. From the Latin of THOMAS A KEMPIS. By the Rt. Rev. BISHOP CHALLONER. In one vol., 32mo., extra cloth, gilt backs.
PRICE—Cloth binding, . . . . . . . . . $0 25
    " gilt edges, . . . . . . . . . . 0 50

**THE FOLLOWING OF CHRIST.** New and beautiful edition. 24mo. Translated from the original Latin of THOMAS A KEMPIS. By the Rt. Rev. BISHOP CHALLONER, with a new translation of a Practical Reflection and Prayer at the end of each chapter. From the French of FATHER DE GONNELIEU, S. J.
,PRICE—Handsome cloth binding, 1 plate, . . . . $0 38
    American morocco, . . . . . . . . 0 50
    " " full gilt edges and sides, 6 plates, . . 0 75
    Turkey " gilt edges, 6 plates, . . . . 1 50
    " " super extra, gilt edges, 8 plates, . . 2 00

**THE COMPLETE WORKS OF ST. ALPHONSUS LIGUORI.** New translation, Edited by Rev. R. A. COFFIN, C.SS.R. The only unabridged edition.
Vol. I. THE CHRISTIAN VIRTUES. AND THE MEANS OF OBTAINING THEM.

VOLUME II.
MEDITATIONS AND DISCOURSES ON THE INCARNATION.

VOLUME III.

VISITS TO THE BLESSED SACRAMENT AND SPIRIT OF ST. LIGUORI.

VOLUME IV.

THE GLORIES OF MARY.

PRICE—Handsome cloth binding, full gilt edges, 2 plates,    .   .   . $1 50
"      "      "   gilt back, 1 plate, .     .   .   .   . 1 00
"      "      "   1 plate, .     .   .   .   .   . 0 75

**VISITS TO THE BLESSED SACRAMENT AND THE BLESSED VIRGIN MARY.**     PRICE—31 cents.

**PRACTICE OF THE LOVE OF OUR LORD JESUS CHRIST.** By ST. ALPHONSUS LIGUORI.     PRICE—31 cents.

**TREATISE ON PRAYER.** By ST. ALPHONSUS LIGUORI.     PRICE—31 cents.

**RULE OF LIFE FOR A CHRISTIAN.** By ST. ALPHONSUS LIGUORI,     PRICE—31 cents.

**SPIRIT OF LIGUORI,**     PRICE—31 cents.

**THE ELEVATION OF THE SOUL TO GOD.** By means of Spiritual Considerations and Affections, Translated from the French of L'ABBE BARAULT. 1 vol. 18mo.
PRICE—Cloth,   .   .   .   .   .   .   .   .   .   .   .   . 50 cents.

**THINK WELL ON'T;** Or Reflections on the Great Truths of the Christian Religion for every day of the Month. By the Rt. Rev. Dr. CHALLONER, D.D. To which is added Devotions to the Sacred Heart of Jesus. 1 vol. 24mo.
PRICE—Cloth gilt,   .   .   .   .   .   .   .   .   . 18¾ cents.

**SPIRITUAL MAXIMS OF ST. VINCENT OF PAUL.** Arranged for every day in the year. By the Most Rev. WM. WALSH, D.D. To which is added, a Nine Days' Devotion, in honor of St. Vincent; and Biographical Notice of Mrs. Seton. Foundress and First Superior of the Sisters of Charity in the United States. 32mo,
PRICE—Cloth,   .   .   .   .   .   .   .   .   .   .   . 25 cents.

**HAY ON MIRACLES.** The Scripture Doctrine of Miracles Displayed. In which their Nature, &c., are Impartially Examined and Explained according to the light of Revelation and the Principles of Sound Reason. 2 vols. 12mo., 2 plates. By the Rt. Rev. GEORGE HAY, D.D.
PRICE—Cloth,   .   .   .   .   .   .   .   .   .   . 75 cents.

**BUTLER'S FEASTS AND FASTS.** The Movable Feasts, Fasts, and other Annual Observances of the Catholic Church. By the Rev. ALBAN BUTLER. 12mo. A treatise on Corpus Christi and the Sacred Heart have been added by an eminent prelate.
PRICE—Cloth,   .   .   .   .   .   .   .   .   . 75 cents.

**THE CATHOLIC CHRISTIAN** Instructed in the Sacraments, Sacrifices, Ceremonies, and Observances of the Church. By the Rev. Dr. CHALLONER. 1 vol.
PRICE—Cloth,   .   .   .   .   .   .   .   .   .   . 25 cents.
Paper,   .   .   .   .   .   .   .   .   .   .   . 18¾ "

**YOUTH'S DIRECTOR;** Or, Familiar Instructions for Young People, with a number of Historical Tracts and Edifying Examples. Translated from the French, by the Rt. Rev. WM. TYLER, Bishop of Hartford. 1 vol. 18mo.
PRICE—Cloth,   .   .   .   .   .   .   .   .   . 31 cents.

**SANCTA SOPHIA;** Or, Directions for the Prayer of Contemplation. By the Rev. AUGUSTINE BAKER, of the Order of St. Benedict. This is the masterpiece of the English Ascetic School.
PRICE—Neat Cloth, .   .   .   .   .   .   .   . $1 00

**HOURS BEFORE THE ALTAR;** Or, Meditations on the Blessed Sacrament. By Mgr. BOUILLERIE. A book of great piety, unction and fervor.
1 Vol. Neat Cloth,   .   .   .   .   .   .   .   . 25 cents.

**THE LOVE OF MARY;** Or, Readings for the Month of May. By Father Roberto. Full of true and genuine piety.
1 Vol. Neat Cloth, .   .   .   .   .   .   .   . 38 cents.

70

# VI. HISTORICAL WORKS, BIOGRAPHY, TRAVELS, &c.

**THE LIFE OF THE BLESSED VIRGIN MARY, OF HER CHASTE SPOUSE ST. JOSEPH, AND HOLY PARENTS ST. JOACHIM AND ST. ANNE.** A most beautiful work, never yet surpassed by the American Press. Specially approved by the Most Rev. JOHN HUGHES, D.D., Archbishop of N. York. The Life of the Blessed Virgin, by Monsignore Emidio Gentilucci, Chamberlain of Honor to His Holiness, dedicated to and honored with the suffrages of Pope Pius IX. The Life of St. Joseph, by Father Ignatius Vallejo, of the Society of Jesus. The Lives of St. Joachim and St. Anne, are by the Jesuit Father Binet, with notes by Father Vallejo.

*Inducement :*—Each subscriber to this splendid work will receive with the last number a magnificent steel engraving, suitable for framing, of the Most Rev. John Hughes, D.D., Archbishop of New York. The work is published in 20 parts at 25 cents each. Every number contains 48 pages of letter-press, with borders, vignettes, and tail pieces of exquisite finish, and one fine steel engraving. It can also be had bound in various styles, at the following prices :—1 vol. 960 pages, 21 steel plates, and over 100 beautiful vignettes on wood :

English cloth, plain, . . . . . . . . $5 75
"      "      gilt, . . . . . . . 6 50
"      morocco, marbled edges, . . . . 6 50
"      "      gilt edges, . . . . . 7 00
Turkey morocco extra, . . . . . . 8 00
"      "      bevelled, . . . . . 9 00
"      "      panelled sides, . . . . . 10 00

**LIFE OF THE BLESSED VIRGIN MARY, MOTHER OF GOD.** Taken from the Traditions of the East, the Manners of the Israelites, and the Writings of the Holy Fathers. From the French of M. L'ABBE ORSINI. By the Rev. PATRICK POWER, D.D. 16mo.

PRICE—Cloth binding, 1 fine engraving, . . . . . . $0 50
"      "      gilt edges, 4 plates, . . . . . 1 00
"      "      full gilt edges and sides, 6 fine plates, . . 1 50

**HISTORY OF THE LIFE AND INSTITUTE OF ST. IGNATIUS LOYOLA,** Founder of the Society of Jesus. Translated from the Italian of Bartoli. By MADAME CALDERON DE LA BARCA, Authoress of "Life in Mexico," &c. 2 vols. small 8vo.

PRICE—English cloth, . . . . . . . . $2 25

**HISTORY OF THE CATHOLIC MISSIONS** among the Indian Tribes of the United States; 1529 –1854. By JOHN GILMARY SHEA, Author of the "Discovery and Exploration of the Mississippi," &c., &c. 1 vol. small 8vo., 6 steel plates and 4 other illustrations.

PRICE—English cloth, . . . . . . . . . . $1 75

**CATHOLIC MISSIONS AND MISSIONARIES.**
PRICE—Flexible cloth, . . . . . . . . . . 19 cents.

**THE CATHOLIC CHURCH IN THE UNITED STATES.** Pages of Its History. By HENRY DE COURCY and JOHN GILMARY SHEA. 1 Vol. 12mo.
PRICE—English cloth, . . . . . . . . . $1 50

**BLOODY MARY AND GOOD QUEEN BESS.** A true history of their reigns, showing which was Good and which was Bloody.
PRICE—Flexible cloth, . . . . . . . . . 25 cents.

**THE CONVERT: OR, LEAVES FROM MY EXPERIENCE.** By O. A. BROWNSON, LL.D. Though not purporting to be an autobiography, it challenges an unusual interest, from being the intellectual history of this eminent philosopher.
PRICE—1 vol. cloth, 450 pages, . . . . . . . . $1 25

**THE HISTORY OF IRELAND,** from its Earliest King to its Last Chief. By THOS. MOORE, Esq. The only American Edition of Moore's most beautiful and classic history of the Isle of Saints.
2 vols. 8vo.—PRICE, . . . . . . . . . . . $4

**ROME: ITS OHURCHES, ITS CHARITIES, AND ITS SCHOOLS.** By Rev. W. H. Neligan, LL.D. A most complete and eloquent description of the Eternal City, which no Catholic family can dispense with.
PRICE—Cloth, 12mo. . . . . . . . . . . . 75 cents.

**MY TRIP TO FRANCE.** By Rev. J. P. Donelan. A lively, sketchy book of travels.
PRICE—Cloth, 12mo. . . . . . . . . . . . 75 cents.

---

# VII. CATHOLIC TALES.

**ITALIAN LEGENDS AND SKETCHES.** By Rev. J. W. Cummings, D.D.
PRICE—1 vol. 12mo. . . . . . . . . . . 75 cents.

**THORNBERRY ABBEY.** A Tale of the Times. By Mrs. Parsons. 1 vol. 18mo.
PRICE—Cloth, gilt back, . . . . . . . . 88 cents.

**THE SHIPWRECK;** Or, the Desert Island.
PRICE—Neat cloth binding, gilt back . . . . . . 88 cents.

**ORAMAIKA;** An Indian Story. A charming little tale from the French.
PRICE—Neat cloth binding, gilt back . . . . . . 50 cents.

**CHATEAU LESCURE;** Or, the Last Marquis. By Donald M'Leod.
PRICE—Neat cloth binding, gilt back . . . . . . 88 cents.

**BLIND AGNESE;** Or, The Little Bride of the Blessed Sacrament. By Cecilia Caddell.
PRICE—Neat cloth, gilt back . . . . . . . 88 cents.

**LITTLE FRANK;** Or, A Painter's Progress; and what a Mother can endure. From the Flemish of Hendrik Conscience. 1 vol. 18mo., profusely illustrated.
PRICE—Cloth binding . . . . . . . . 87½ cents.

**FASHION;** Or, Siska Van Roosemael. From the Flemish of Hendrik Conscience. 18mo. With thirty-five illustrations.
PRICE—Cloth binding . . . . . . . . 87½ cents

**SCHMID'S EXQUISITE TALES.**
Superbly illustrated from original designs by the distinguished American artist, J. G. Chapman, and executed in the highest style of the art of wood engraving, in 5 vols. 88 cents a vol. Gilt edges, . . . . . . . . 75 cents.

Separate Tales in cloth or in paper, from 6 to 25 cents.

**THE YOUNG CRUSADERS.** PRICE, . . . . 88 cents.

**CONSCIENCE;** Or, the Trials of May Brook. By Mrs. A. H. Dorsey. 2 vols.
PRICE, . . . . . . . . . . . . 75 cents.

**THE HAMILTONS;** Or, Sunshine and Storm. By Cora Berkeley.
PRICE, . . . . . . . . . . . . 88 cents.

**THE THREE ELEANORS.** By the Authoress of the Hamiltons.
PRICE, . . . . . . . . . . . . 68 cents.

**LIZZIE MAITLAND.** By Mrs. D. W. C. Clarke. Edited by O. A. Brownson, D.D.
PRICE, . . . . . . . . . . . . 68 cents.

**AILEY MOORE.** By Father Baptist. 2 vols.
PRICE, . . . . . . . . . . . . 75 cents.

**THE PROPHET OF THE RUINED ABBEY;** Or, A Glance at the Future of Ireland. Founded on the Prophecies of Culmkill. 1 vol. 12mo.
PRICE—Cloth, gilt . . . . . . . . . 50 cents.

72

## VIII. CATHOLIC SCHOOL-BOOKS,

*Published under the approbation of the Most Rev. John Hughes, D.D ,*
*Archb'p of N.York.*

DUNIGAN & BROTHER invite the attention of the Catholic Clergy, Colleges, Convents, and Parish Schools, to their large, cheap, and durable CLASS BOOKS, unsurpassed in any particular by any published in the country. Many of these works have been got up expressly for this country, and the others have been improved and adapted by able and well-known Catholic writers.

Copies for examination sent gratuitously, and free of postage, on application. A large discount allowed to Schools and Colleges.

| | | | |
|---|---|---|---|
| 1.—CATHOLIC PRIMER. | . . . . . . | PRICE—6 cents. |
| 2.—THE PRACTICAL SPELLING-BOOK . | . . | " 12½ cts. |
| 3.—CARPENTER'S SPELLER'S ASSISTANT. | . . | " 12½ cts. |
| 4.—THE CATHOLIC SCHOOL BOOK. | . . . | " 15 cents. |
| 5.—WALKER'S DICTIONARY. Only unexceptionable Ed. | | " 50 do. |
| 6.—LESSONS FOR YOUNG LEARNERS. No. 1. | | " 6½ cents. |
| 7.— " " " No. 2. | | " 12½ cents. |

Admirable little readers.

CHRISTIAN BROTHERS' BOOKS. Specially sanctioned and approved by the Provincial of the Brothers in this country.

| | | | |
|---|---|---|---|
| 8.—FIRST BOOK. Cheap edition. | . . . . . | PRICE 4 cents. |
| 9.—SECOND BOOK. " " | . . . . . | " 10 do. |
| 10.—THIRD BOOK. " " | . . . . . | " 38 do. |
| 11.—FIRST BOOK, Improved edition. . | . . . . | " 6½ do. |
| 12.—SECOND BOOK. " " | . . . . . | " 12½ cts. |
| 13.—THIRD BOOK. Improved Edition. | . . . . | " 50 do. |
| 14.—FOURTH BOOK. " " | . . . . . | " 68 do. |

DUNIGAN & BROTHERS alone issue the *complete* series of Christian Brothers' Books; and their editions are superior to any others in every respect.

15.—THE UNIVERSAL READING BOOK. Justly and extensively admired.

PRICE—37½ cents.

| | | | |
|---|---|---|---|
| 16.—CHALLONER'S BIBLE HISTORY. | . . . . | . " 31 do. |
| 17.—GRACE'S OUTLINES OF HISTORY. | . . | " 31 do. |
| 18.—SHEA'S HISTORY OF MODERN EUROPE. | . | " 75 do. |
| 19.—SHEA'S HISTORY OF THE UNITED STATES. | | " 31 do. |
| 20.—SELECTA EX CLASSICIS AUCTORIBUS I. | | |

Containing Viri Romæ, Phædrus, Selections from Cicero, &c.     25 do.

21.—SELECTA EX CLASSICIS AUCTORIBUS II.

Containing Nepos, Phædrus, De Senectute, Selections,'&c.   " 87 do.

| | | | |
|---|---|---|---|
| 22.—VIRI ROMÆ. By LHOMOND. | . . . . . | " 25 do. |
| 23.—PHÆDRUS, FABULAE. | . . . . . | " 18 do. |
| 24.—CORNELIUS NEPOS, VITÆ IMPERATORUM. | " 25 do. |
| 25.—CICERO DE SENECTUTE. | . ' . . . | " 12 do. |